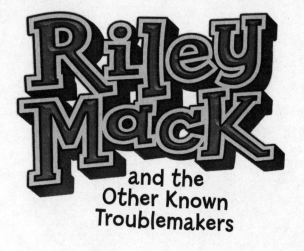

Riley Mack

and the
Other Known
Troublemakers

Riley Mack

and the
Other Known
Troublemakers

CHRIS GRABENSTEIN

HARPER
An Imprint of HarperCollinsPublishers

Library of Congress Cataloging-in-Publication Data
Grabenstein, Chris.
Riley Mack and the other known troublemakers / by Chris
Grabenstein. — 1st ed.
    p. cm.
Summary: Twelve-year-old Riley Mack and his friends
Briana, Mongo, Jake, and Jamal outwit the school bully, solve
the mystery of who stole the goldendoodle named Noodle, and
get evidence to help the FBI catch bank robbers.
  ISBN 978-0-06-202620-0 (trade bdg.)
  [1. Heroes—Fiction. 2. Bullies—Fiction. 3. Schools—Fiction. 4.
Friendship—Fiction. 5. Embezzlement—Fiction. 6. Robbers and
outlaws—Fiction. 7. Mystery and detective stories.] I. Title.
PZ7.G7487Ri 2012   2011016616
[Fic]—dc23   CIP
                                                            AC
Typography by Erin Fitzsimmons
12 13 14 15 16   CG/RRDH   10 9 8 7 6 5 4 3 2 1
❖

First Edition

FOR TOM, JEFF, STEVE, & BILL—
MY BROTHERS AND
THE ORIGINAL TROUBLEMAKERS

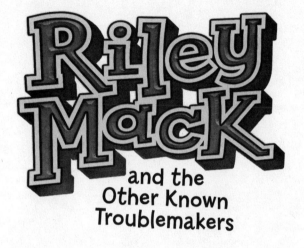

and the
Other Known
Troublemakers

SCHOOL WAS FINISHED FOR THE week and Riley Mack
was itching for some action.

It was early May. Spring and mischief were in the air.

Riley and two of his best buds were sitting in their
regular booth at the Pizza Palace on Main Street. Riley
had already rearranged the letters on the pizzeria's
sidewalk reader board from "Buy One Get One Free"
to "Neon Beef Eye Grout." That was fun, for like sixty
seconds.

Now he and Mongo were playing pizza crust football.

"So Trystan Bordeau reached out to me today," said
Riley. He flicked his finger at a chunk of crust, sending
it flying over to Mongo, whose real name was Hubert

Montgomery but since he was so humongous (freakishly larger than any twelve-year-old in the known universe), Riley, and, therefore, everybody else, called him Humongo—Mongo for short.

Mongo finger-kicked the crust back to Riley's plate. "What'd he want?"

"For us to break into the school this weekend. Steal the answer key to his geometry final."

"What'd you tell him?" asked Jake Lowenstein, the third member of Riley's after-school crew. Jake was too focused on thumbing out a text message to look up from his cell phone.

Riley grinned. "That we don't play that way on account of the brain surgery I might need in thirty, forty years."

"Huh?" Mongo looked confused.

"Riley was creating a hypothetical scenario," said Jake. As always, he was wearing his brown dragon-print hoodie with the lid up and kind of looked like a monk-warrior from a ninja movie. He was way smarter than Riley (or anyone else who had ever been in the seventh grade at Fairview Middle School), so he could use words like *hypothetical* and *scenario*.

"Oh," said Mongo, still confused.

Riley helped Mongo out: "I told Trystan, 'What if, when I get old, I forget to wear my helmet and fall off my bike? You think I want to be operated on by a

2

brain surgeon who cheated his way through middle and medical school?'"

"Good answer," said Jake. Now his smartphone made a funny rumbling noise. Sounded like it was popping armpit farts.

"That's my new text tone," he said, checking out his screen. "Uh-oh. Briana needs us. Immediately."

"Where is she?" said Riley, sitting up straight and feeling his brain start buzzing. Maybe this was the action he'd been waiting for.

"Two blocks away. Quick Pick Mini Mart. Corner of Old Post Road and Sanford Street."

"Situation?"

"Fifth grader being harassed by Gavin Brown."

Mongo's face went to code purple because the big guy despised bullies. "Brown?" He sledgehammered both his fists on the tabletop. The Parmesan and hot-pepper-flake shakers shook. "I thought that doofus graduated."

"He did," said Riley with disgust. "He's a freshman over at the high school."

"So what's he doing harassing a fifth grader?"

"Guess he came back to pick on someone who *isn't* his own size. Makes the tough guy act a lot easier to pull off when your victims don't punch back." Riley sensed his dull Friday was about to become extremely interesting. He got a devilish twinkle in his eye. "So,

3

Jake—do we know this fifth grader?"

"Nope. Briana says he's a newbie."

Riley nodded. His wheels were spinning. He loved using his wits to go up against the big, the bad, and the Gavin Browns. "We know anybody on the inside? What's the adult interference situation?"

"Hang on," said Jake, swiping his fingers back and forth across the glass face of his tweaked-out smartphone. "Accessing security cameras."

Riley was impressed. "You can do that?"

"Only with CCTVs tied to the net."

"CCTV?" said Mongo. "I don't think we get that channel."

"CCTV means closed-circuit TV," explained Jake. "Security cameras. Fortunately, all the Quick Pick shops feed their video into a centralized server."

"Cool." Riley leaned back. Let Jake's fingers work their magic.

"Okay, this is good. Mr. Karpinksi is behind the counter."

The name sounded familiar. Riley stroked his chin. "Karpinksi, Karpinski . . ."

Mongo rubbed the stubble on top of his huge head. "Karpinksi . . ."

"Mr. Alexander Karpinksi," said Jake. "Day manager of the Quick Pick. We helped his son, Alex Junior, out of a similar jam last year. Basketball game. The bully under the bleachers? You orchestrated that fifty-person popcorn-box dump. Remember, Riley? Freaked the butt head out, big-time."

"Oh, yeah," said Riley, relishing the memory. "That was a good one."

"One of your best," said Mongo.

Riley shrugged modestly. "It did the job."

"Briana says, 'RUUP4IT?'"

"Works for me," said Riley. "You guys in?"

"Definitely," said Jake.

"Totally," said Mongo. "But, well, I have to be home by five thirty to walk the dog."

Now Riley looked confused. "Dog? What dog?"

"Noodle. She's our new goldendoodle puppy. She cost my mom fifteen hundred dollars."

Riley's jaw dropped. Jake turtled his head out of his hoodie. Even Nick, the Pizza Palace delivery guy, who was clearing the table in the next booth, dropped his tub of dirty dishes in disbelief.

"Fifteen hundred bucks?" said Riley. "For a dog?"

"Well," said Mongo, "Noodle is very cute. Sort of like a teddy bear with a tail."

Jake's smartphone armpit-farted again.

"Uh-oh," he said. "Briana reports 'the situation is deteriorating.' Gavin Brown is now jamming the little guy's head into the freezer case."

"That does it!" Mongo exploded. "I'm gonna sit on

Brown's chest and pound his face!"

Riley placed a gentle hand on Mongo's furiously clenched fist. "Take it easy. We don't need Gavin Brown to be afraid of you. We need him to be afraid of this fifth grader."

"Good luck with that," said Jake. "On the security camera feed, the kid looks like he weighs less than a frozen burrito. Saving him from Brown is going to be tough."

Riley smiled confidently. "Tough, my friend, is what we do best. Tell Briana we're on our way. We'll go with the Payoff Protection play. We'll need some ketchup, syrup, and cash. Have her clue in Mr. Karpinksi. Feed him his lines. Shut down the shop."

Jake's fingers tap-danced across the smartphone's face. "Done and done."

Riley gestured at the hunk of crust on his otherwise empty paper plate. "You want it, Mongo?"

"Nah. I want Gavin Brown!"

"Then let's roll."

RILEY, MONGO, AND JAKE RAN three abreast up the sidewalk, their JanSport backpacks slapping against their spines in time to their strides.

They heard a whistle. The two-fingered, big-city kind that can stop traffic. Train traffic.

"Yo, Riley! You guys! Over here."

It was Briana Bloomfield, standing in the parking lot of the Quick Pick Mini Mart, windmilling her arms over her head. She was wearing a bright red wig, some kind of billowy silk scarf, and rhinestone-studded sunglasses. Briana was big on theatrics. She *loved* (just about everything she said came out in italics) wearing costumes and pretending to be somebody she wasn't.

"Who are you supposed to be?" asked Mongo, his eyes wide with awe.

"It's a disguise!" gushed Briana. "I didn't want Gavin to know it was *me* following him!"

"So you put on a clown wig and flashy glasses?" asked Jake.

"Exactly!" said Briana. "Would someone who was tailing you wear a costume so ridiculously conspicuous? No. They'd try to blend in. Hide in plain sight. They sure wouldn't dress like this! Gavin Brown never knew I was following him!"

Amused, Riley examined Briana's blazingly bright Bozo wig and shook his head. Riley himself had shaggy red hair but his was the orangish color of fox fur, not the freakish color of a fire truck.

"How we doing inside?" he asked.

"We're on script," said Briana. "Mr. Karpinksi's behind the counter, yelling, 'Stop, stop,' threatening to call the cops. Gavin keeps pummeling the little guy, trying to snag his iPod, shake him down for cash."

"And the fifth grader won't give in?"

"Nope."

Riley slipped off his backpack. "I like this new kid already." He unzipped the bag's main compartment.

"We need to hurry," said Briana, whipping off her bedazzled shades. "Gavin's giving the guy a freezy wheezy."

"Is that like a triple nipple cripple or ruby booby?" asked Jake, who had, apparently, studied Bully Lingo 101.

"No," said Briana. "He has the kid's face stuffed in the freezer—right above the microwavable breakfast biscuits and Hot Pockets."

Riley pulled two handy-talky radios out of his backpack, powered them up, and tossed one to Briana. "You give Mr. Karpinksi your cell number?" he asked Briana.

"Check!"

"When he calls, you know what to do."

"Yep. But I might try a new voice or two, okay?"

"Fine. Just make it work."

"Oh, I will." She pointed a finger to the sky and proclaimed, "There are no small parts, only small actors!"

"Right."

"I also locked down the set." Briana gestured toward the Quick Pick's sliding glass doors. The Sorry We're Closed sign was flipped into place. "We have total control of the store. No grown-ups, in or out."

"Excellent." Riley tossed the second battery-powered radio to Jake. "Once Mongo and I have Brown's attention, slip in, stay low, and head behind the counter. When Mr. Karpinksi calls the cops, go to channel B."

"Got it. You want me to make it squeal and stuff?"

"Can you do that?" asked Briana.

"Boo-yeah!" said Jake.

The other three stared at him.

"Sorry," he said, retreating inside his hoodie. "Just a little pumped, you know?"

"Definitely," said Riley. "I'm right there with you. Mongo, if you don't mind, mess up your shirt a little."

Mongo popped open a button, tugged his shirttail out of his pants. "Like this?"

"Perfect." Riley turned to Briana. "You grab the ketchup and pancake syrup packs off the condiment counter?"

"Boo-yeah!"

Now everybody stared at *her*.

"Sorry." She pulled a small plastic tub from her backpack. "I mixed it up already." The ketchup was for color. The syrup thickened it up and sold the slop as coagulating blood.

Mongo took the tub. "Where should I put it, Riley?"

"Nose and mouth. Make it look like someone gave you a bad bone taco."

"A what?"

"A punch in the face."

"Oh." Mongo dabbed his finger in the thick red goop.

Briana put a hand to her hip. "Have you ever worn makeup before, Mongo?"

"Once. For Halloween. I was a werewolf and glued teddy bear fuzz to my face."

"Come here," said Briana. She found a cotton swab in her makeup kit and used it to paint a line of fake blood dribbling down from the corner of Mongo's lips. Then she stuffed a thick gob of the ketchup concoction up his left nostril. "Let your schnozzle drip. Just like you do in the winter."

Mongo nodded. "Okay." The nodding made red goop splatter down the front of his shirt. Briana jammed another swab of the crimson crud up his snout.

"Don't shake your head again until you guys are inside, okay?"

"Okay," said Mongo, catching himself this time before he nodded.

Briana balled up her fist. "You need me to punch you in the face so you can totally feel the pain?"

"No, thanks," said Mongo. "I'm good."

"Mr. Karpinksi lend you the cash?" asked Riley.

Briana handed him a stack of twenty-dollar bills. "Two hundred bucks."

"Works for me."

"He, of course, wants it back. I mean, he's grateful we saved Alex Junior last year but he's not *that* grateful."

"No problem. We're not in this for the money."

"Um," said Jake as he fiddled with the portable radio, "you ever think about adjusting that portion of the Riley Mack credo?"

"No," Riley said. "Why?"

"Well, money for a new Guitar Hero might be nice," said Mongo.

Jake nodded. "Or a flash drive."

"I need a new pair of vampire fangs," said Briana.

"You guys?" said Riley, cocking up his left eyebrow.

"Sorry," the other three said in unison.

Riley rubbed his hands together. He was ready to do this thing. "We know the fifth grader's name?"

"Wilson," said Briana. "Jamal Wilson. And Riley?"

"Yeah?"

"Hurry up. With his head buried in the deep freeze, the poor kid looks like an eighty-pound sack of human ice cubes!"

RILEY LED THE WAY THROUGH the Quick Pick Mini Mart's sliding glass doors.

Mongo stumbled in behind him and started moaning, "Oh, my face. He punched me in my face. Jamal gave me a bone taco."

Riley figured Mongo wouldn't win best actor in his category this year, but he was doing just fine. The gentle giant was totally focused, like he always was whenever they set out to take down a bully—even though back in fifth grade, when Riley first met Mongo, everybody thought Mongo *was* the class bully because he was so immense and would seriously mess up anybody dumb enough to make fun of the teddy bear trinkets he had dangling off the zipper of his backpack. One day, in the cafeteria, Riley gave Mongo his snack pack of Teddy Grahams cookies. Chocolatey Chip flavor. They talked. Riley suggested that maybe Mongo should redirect his rage. Mongo said he'd give it a try if people quit making fun of his teddy bears, which Riley said he'd take care of. They'd been pals ever since.

Now Riley led Mongo to a spot where his bulk would block Gavin Brown's view while Jake scampered off to hide behind the checkout counter.

"That does it!" shouted Mr. Karpinksi, the manager. "I'm calling the cops!"

"Fine," bellowed Gavin. He looked like somebody had dropped him out of his crib face-first, leaving him with a flat nose, flatter eyes, and a permanent smirk plastered on his flat lips. Sort of like a flounder with a bad attitude. "Go ahead. Call the police! They'll be on my side. They always are!"

"Wow!" said Riley. He and Mongo waltzed up the potato chip, CornNuts, and beef jerky aisle toward the freezer cases. "Is that Jamal Wilson?"

"What?" Gavin twisted around, keeping one arm locked on the scrawny fifth grader's skull. Riley could see that the kid was shivering. "Who the heck are you?"

Riley gave Gavin a brisk two-finger salute off the tip of his eyebrow. "Riley Mack. We've met."

"Oh, yeah. You're the punk who's always looking out for the losers. What're you doing here, punk?"

"Trying to protect *you*, Gavin."

"What?"

"When you call the cops, Mr. Karpinski," Riley shouted over his shoulder, "let them know we found Jamal Wilson."

"Okay!"

Riley could hear the manager beeping out a phone number. Sure, it had more notes than 911 should, but Riley was banking on the fact that Brown, being a bully, was likely an idiot, too. Probably had trouble counting above one and two.

"Hello?" he heard Mr. Karpinski say. "Is this the police?" It came out stilted, but Briana had only fed him his lines, like, five minutes ago.

Gavin laughed. "I told you wimps—I'm not afraid of the cops."

"They're not coming to get *you*, pal," said Riley. "They want *him*." He gestured toward the flailing legs dangling out of the freezer case.

"What?"

"That's Jamal Wilson!"

"So?"

Riley nodded toward Mongo. "You know my man Mongo?"

One of Gavin Brown's sunken eyeballs twitched;

probably remembering the last time Mongo sat on his chest and flicked at his earlobes.

"Yeah. I know Mongo. The teddy bear freak. What happened to his face?"

"Jamal Wilson!" said Riley.

"This wuss? No way. This skinny little wiener is a walking vending machine. I hit him up for two iPods last week. Now he's got a brand-new one and it's got my name on it, too."

"No it d-d-doesn't!" came a muffled voice from inside the freezer case. "It's m-m-my dad's!" Riley figured the kid was shuddering out of frostbite as much as fear.

"Shut up! I want his cell phone and cash, too! He coughs 'em up, maybe I let him live."

Riley chuckled, shaking his head from side to side. He was enjoying this. "Gavin, Gavin, Gavin. Will you never learn?"

"Learn what?"

"I told you: that's Jamal Wilson!"

"So?"

"*The* Jamal Wilson?"

"Am I supposed to know him or something?"

"New kid in town, am I right, Jamal?"

"Y-y-yes!"

"Featherweight Golden Gloves champion. Three years running. Right, Jamal?"

"W-w-w . . ."

"His fists are registered as lethal weapons. Isn't that right, Jamal?"

"I-I-I don't . . ."

". . . wanna talk about it? Of course you don't. On account of what you did back in Pinedale. You remember Pinedale, don't you Jamal?"

"I-I-I . . ."

Riley moved in close on Gavin. "His family had to move here because Jamal kept getting kicked out of schools. Pinedale, Poughkeepsie, Pittsburgh, Paducah . . ."

"Piscataway!" added Mongo, who must've thought they were playing some kind of alphabetical geography game.

"A lot of places," Riley said quickly. "And, yes, the Wilson family prefers towns that start with the letter *P*."

Gavin raised his eyebrows with interest. "Why'd they kick him out of all those schools?"

"Incorrigible fisticuffs."

"Huh?"

"He knocked out too many kids with his bare knuckles. Took down some teachers, too. Sent a principal to the hospital!"

Gavin laughed. "This little worm?"

"That's right. He's wormy. He slithers into a new

17

town. Lets everybody think he's a wimp. Strings you along. Then, bam! He sucker punches the toughest kids in town, takes over their territory. Tell Gavin how it went down with you, Mongo."

Mongo pointed to his bloody nose and lip. "He did all this with one punch."

Now a radio started squealing and screeching. There was even some feedback. Under the checkout counter, Jake Lowenstein was working his technomagic.

"That sounds like my police scanner!" said Mr. Karpinski, who had memorized his lines perfectly.

"*One Adam-Twelve, One Adam-Twelve*," squawked a very nasal police dispatcher as played by Briana Bloomfield out in the parking lot with her handy talky. "*See the man. Quick Pick Mini Mart. We have Jamal Wilson cornered in the frozen food department. Approach with extreme caution.*"

"Who's that?" asked Gavin, a hint of panic in his voice. "That's not the dispatcher!"

"Mr. Karpinski called the *state* police," said Riley.

"I thought he was calling the Fairview Police Department!"

"No way," said Riley. "This is a job for the Staties!"

"*One Adam-Twelve requesting backup,*" came a new voice over the radio. This time Briana sounded like an angry man with a nasty frog in his throat. "*Listen, sister—if you expect us to apprehend and arrest Jamal*

Wilson, we're gonna need the SWAT team! Tell them to bring their biggest bazooka! Tell them to bring a tank! Tell them to say their prayers!"

Riley pulled out the wad of cash Mr. Karpinski had loaned them. Started peeling off bills. "What's it going to take for you to leave my friend Mongo alone, Wilson? Huh? One hundred? Two hundred?"

Gavin's jaw dropped. *"You're* paying *him* off?"

Mongo took one step forward. "It is the only way for me. To walk the streets. Without constantly looking. Over my shoulder. In fear!" Mongo usually memorized his part of a script in chunks.

Riley stuffed the money into the short kid's trembling fist.

"Enjoy, Jamal. You might consider paying him off, too, Gavin. After all, now he knows your name is Gavin Brown. And I wouldn't be surprised if he knew that you live at Forty-eight Crestwood Drive."

"So?"

"He'll hunt you down like a dog and hurt you, Gavin. He'll hurt you bad!"

Gavin finally took his hand off Jamal's head, which was still stuffed between tubs of ice cream. "No way. My dad won't let Jamal Wilson or anybody else hurt me."

"Your dad, my dad—they can't be everywhere every minute of every day, can they?"

Gavin shook his head. "No. They can't." He gulped once. Then his fishy eyes nearly popped out of his face in fear. "I gotta go!"

Breaking into a run, legs flailing, he scuttled backward up the snack aisle. He banged into a big cardboard display and sent several dozen candy bars skittering across the floor.

"Daddy!" they heard him scream from out in the parking lot. "Daddy!"

Riley tapped Jamal Wilson on the shoulder.

"It's okay, kid. He's gone. You can pull your head out of the freezer."

"I'm thuck."

"What?"

"I'm thuck. My thongue."

MEANWHILE, A FEW BLOCKS SOUTH of the Quick Pick, Riley's mom, Mrs. Madiera Mack, was gearing up for the Friday afternoon rush at the First National Bank of Fairview on Main Street.

It was 4:30 p.m. and Mrs. Mack, who worked at the bank as a teller, knew the lobby would soon be crowded with folks eager to cash their weekly paychecks—just like it was every Friday after five.

"Good afternoon, Maddie."

It was her manager, Chuck "call me Chip" Weitzel. He was about the same age as Riley's mom, maybe thirty-five, and carried himself like the swaggering college football star he used to be. His smile was so syrupy sweet, it made Mrs. Mack's teeth hurt.

"Busy?" he asked.

"Not yet."

The bank manager checked his watch. "Rush hour will be starting soon. Let me slide in here, give you a break." .

"That's okay, Mr. Weitzel. I can handle it."

"Please, Maddie—call me Chip."

He told her that every time they talked but Mrs. Mack didn't want to call him, or any other middle-aged man, "Chip."

"Of course my working your teller window is in no way a reflection on the fantastic job you're doing for FNBOF."

Only he pronounced it "Fin-boff."

"Every now and then," he continued, "I just like to take over a teller cage and spend some quality time with our customers."

But why does it always have to be my window? Riley's mom wondered as "Chip" continued his spiel.

"Working the window gives me a chance to listen and respond to the voice of our consumers. . . ."

Apparently, that last bit was something Mr. Weitzel had learned in business school. Riley's mom never went to business school. In fact, she had never even gone to college. Instead, right out of high school, she'd married Riley's dad and set out to "see the world."

Riley's father was in the military.

Mrs. Mack stepped aside. Mr. Weitzel spritzed his mouth with an aerosol blast of minty freshness and moved up to the brass bars of the old-fashioned teller cage.

A sweet little old lady, one of Mrs. Mack's regulars, toddled up to the window.

"Good afternoon, ma'am," said Chip.

"Good afternoon, Maddie."

"Um, Mrs. Rollison?" Riley's mom waved over her boss's shoulder. "Yoo-hoo. I'm over here."

"Oh, hello, dearie. These darn glasses. All I see are shadows and lumps."

"Mrs. Rollison, I'm the bank manager. Chuck Weitzel. I'm filling in for Mrs. Mack this afternoon."

"Oh."

"And please—call me Chip."

"Okay, Chick."

"Chip."

"I'm Rada Rollison." Mrs. Rollison was elderly, hard of hearing, nearly blind, and so short that all Riley's mom ever saw when she came to her window was a fluffy cloud of pinkish white hair.

"Well, *Mr.* Rollison is certainly a lucky young man," said Mr. Weitzel with a wink. "To have such a beautiful bride!"

"Mr. Rollison passed away in January," Riley's mom whispered quickly.

23

Mr. Weitzel kept smiling. "I mean he used to be lucky . . . before he died . . . that wasn't very lucky . . . the dying bit. . . ."

Mrs. Rollison, deaf to everything the bank manager mumbled, hoisted an envelope stuffed with cash up to the counter. "I'd like to deposit this two thousand dollars in my savings account, if you please."

"No problem." He stamped the deposit slip, handed her the pink copy. "You have a great weekend, okay?"

"Why, thank you, Chick."

As Mrs. Rollison tottered away, Mr. Weitzel slipped her envelope, fat with cash, into the teller drawer.

"Um, you didn't count it," said Riley's mom.

"Come again?"

"Her deposit. You didn't match what she gave you with what she wrote down on her deposit slip."

"Good eye." He folded his arms across his chest and smiled, the way a crocodile does before he bites your leg off. "So, Maddie—how's your boy?"

"Riley? Fine."

"I take it he's staying out of trouble?"

"Mr. Weitzel, my son hasn't been in trouble for a long, long time."

"What about that shoplifting thing?"

"That was three years ago. Right after his dad left. He hasn't done anything like it since."

"Still, shoplifting is what the police call a gateway

crime. Leads to bigger felonies down the line. That's why Chief Brown calls Riley a KTM."

"A what?" A KTM sounded like a cash machine for kittens.

"Known Troublemaker. They have his mug shot up at the police station."

"His *mug shot*?"

"Well, maybe it's his class photo. He *is* smiling. People don't usually smile for their mug shots. Anyway, redheaded Riley is right there, smack-dab in the middle of the bulletin board."

"Mr. Weitzel, my son paid for what he tried to steal. He was punished."

"Good, good. Guess it's awfully hard rearing a boy without a man around the house, huh?"

"Riley talks to his father almost every night."

"You worked that out?"

"Yes."

"Good, good." The bank manager spritzed some more minty freshness into his mouth. "So, where's Riley now?"

"With his friends. Down the street at the Pizza Palace. Doing his homework."

"Awesome. So, you wouldn't mind working a little late tonight, right?"

"Well, we were planning on . . ."

"I need to catch a plane. Bank manager conference out west."

"But . . ."

He pulled the teller drawer out from under the counter.

"Tell you what—I'll count out your tray; you take care of whatever comes in over the next hour, then lock up at six." He flashed her his high beam smile.

"But . . ."

"Deal?"

Riley's mom smiled back. Her beams weren't nearly as bright.

"Deal," she said.

Unfortunately, she needed this job. She needed her paycheck more than anything in the world, except, of course, Riley's dad coming home. Alive. From Afghanistan.

RILEY USED A CUP OF warm water from the coffee and tea bar to help Jamal Wilson loosen his tongue from the icy grip of the metal freezer racks.

Even though Jamal's fingers were nearly frozen into french fries, he kept fidgeting with some kind of tiny screwdriver gizmo sticking out of his miniature Swiss Army knife.

"That was awesome!" howled Mongo, wiping his face clean with a napkin from the hot dog counter. "I thought Gavin was going to pee his pants!" Mongo was laughing so hard that he snorted fake blood up his nose.

Jake hopped over the counter with his handheld

radio. "Excellently played, Riley! You okay, kid?"

"Y-y-yeah," said Jamal, his teeth chattering. "N-n-n-now."

"Here you go," said Jake, peeling off his insulated hoodie, a garment he rarely removed because he had cowlick issues—a bad case of kindergarten-nap hair. "I believe, right now, you need this even more than me."

"Th-th-thanks."

Jake draped the sweatshirt over Jamal's shoulders, while the kid kept working on something where the freezer door met the side of the case.

"You guys are good," added Mr. Karpinski.

"Thank you, Mr. K.," said Riley. He was feeling good.

"Y-y-yo, Mr. K.?" stammered Jamal. "While I was spending f-f-face time in your f-f-freezer, I noticed the door h-hinges were a little loose so I m-m-made some adjustments. Loose hinges could s-s-seriously throw off the t-t-toggle switch contacts and make your evaporator f-f-fan run even w-w-when the door is open."

And then he shivered some more. His teeth chattered.

Riley, Jake, and Mongo stared at the little dude in surprise. Mr. Karpinski nodded, impressed.

"Thank you, Jamal."

"My p-p-pleasure."

"So, Riley," said Mr. Karpinski, "is this how you guys rescued Alex Junior?"

"Same basic principle, sir," said Riley. "Bullies are cowards. They just need to be reminded of that fact from time to time."

Briana burst into the store. "That was so incredibly fabtastic! Did you like my second cop? That's the first time I ever did that voice. Was it okay?"

"It was 'fabtastic,'" said Riley.

"You're sure?"

"You were great, Briana," said Jake.

"I thought you were really two people," said Mongo, his mouth full of hot dog. The three pepperoni slices he'd had at the Pizza Palace weren't enough to hold him over till dinner. "Oh, I think I forgot to pay for this," he said to Mr. Karpinski, examining the half of the hot dog he hadn't chomped off with his first bite.

Mr. Karpinski waved it away. "Today, Mongo, the hot dogs are on me!"

Riley took back the wad of cash he had stuffed into Jamal's hand. "You did good, kid."

"W-w-who exactly are you?" asked Jamal.

"Riley Mack."

"Why'd you rescue me from that boofnut?"

"Because we heard you needed rescuing." They shook hands. To Riley, Jamal's fist felt colder than a frozen corn dog. "Mr. Karpinski? How much for hot cocoa?"

"Oh, I don't know, Riley. How about two hundred dollars?"

Riley handed the shopkeeper back his stack of money. "Deal."

Jake pumped Jamal a steaming cup of hot chocolate from a canister dispenser and handed it to him. Still shivering, Jamal took it gratefully.

"Sorry about the collateral damage, Mr. K.," said Riley, surveying the knocked-down candy bar display. "We won't leave until we clean up our mess." He began picking up the less damaged bars, stuffing them into his pockets so he could tote them back to their crunkled rack.

"I really was good, wasn't I?" Briana said to Mongo as they helped Riley tidy up. Like most actresses, Briana needed a ton of praise. Constantly. Standing ovations whenever possible.

"You were incredible," said Mongo. "When I heard you on the radio, I thought you really were the police."

"That's because I, like, so totally believed it! Acting is believing, Mongo. Remember that." She pulled a fluttering hand down in front of her face, closed her eyes, and bowed.

"Okay," said Mongo, who always looked a little spooked whenever Briana flew into cornflake mode.

"How we doing over there?" Riley asked Jake, who was pumping the semifrozen fifth grader a second cup of cocoa.

"Better," said Jake. "I think he's almost thawed."

"You want I should call an ambulance?" asked Mr. Karpinski.

"No need," said Jamal. "I feel fine. And my face is still symmetrical even though my nose was completely crushed against the freezer rack. You know what that word *symmetrical* means?"

"No," said Mongo.

"Means both sides look the same. I memorized that word. I memorized a whole mess of *S* words out of the dictionary last night. *Symmetrical. Symphonic. Symbiotic.* That's two dissimilar organisms living together."

Riley smiled. The new kid had spunk. He was also kind of chatty once his tongue wasn't frozen.

A bell dinged. Somebody had just pulled up to the self-serve gas pumps out in the parking lot.

"Thanks again for the use of your store, Mr. K.," said Riley.

"Hey, you kids did a good thing." Mr. Karpinksi gestured toward Jamal, who was so tiny that the waist of Jake's hooded sweatshirt was hanging below his knees. "Somebody's gotta look out for the little guys, you know what I'm saying?"

"I am not little," said Jamal. "I am diminutive. Do you know what *diminutive* means?"

"Yeah," said Riley. "Little."

The front doors slid open.

"Well, well, well. If it isn't Riley Mack and his annoying little gnat pack."

It was Gavin Brown's father.

"Afternoon, chief," said Mr. Karpinski.

Yep. Gavin Brown's father was the chief of police in Fairview Township. That's why Gavin never worried when anybody threatened to call the cops on him. It just meant his dad would come pick him up and give him a ride home.

Chief Brown tucked his cop hat under his arm and waded into the store. He was a big root beer barrel of a man, filled with nearly as much gas.

"Karpy? Where's my coffee?" the chief called to Mr. Karpinski, never taking his beady eyes off Riley. Coolly, Riley continued picking up candy bars and stuffing them into his pockets.

"Coming right up, chief."

"Two creams and four sugars. And toss in a couple of those doughnuts I like."

The whole time he barked out his order, the chief kept his rat eyes glued on Riley.

Riley stood up. Dusted off his jeans.

"You shoplifting again, Mr. Mack?"

"Nope."

"What's with all those candy bars stuffed in your pockets?"

"He's helping me clean up," said Mr. Karpinski.

"That's my job," said the police chief. "Cleaning up this town's trash."

"Do you, by any chance, mean me, sir?" said Riley. On the inside he felt himself beginning to get mad, but another of his many mottoes was to never let his anger show. He smiled in a friendly way at the chief.

"If the shoe fits, wear it."

"You're mixing your metaphors."

"What?"

"Trash, shoes. You should dance with the horse you rode in on."

The chief fumed. "Karpy, is my coffee ready?"

"Yes, sir."

"Good. And gimme *four* of those doughnuts."

"Right away, chief."

The chief swaggered toward Riley.

Riley kept smiling. He wasn't afraid of the big blowhard just because he had a badge pinned to the chest of his shirt—a shirt that was straining at the buttons. His dad always told Riley, "Fear gives a small thing a big shadow." It would give a blob like Chief Brown a shadow the size of a blimp.

"Who vandalized this store, Mr. Karpinski?" Chief Brown asked, gesturing toward the broken cardboard display. "Was it Riley Mack?"

"Nobody 'vandalized' the store," said the manager as he plunked four doughnuts into a white paper bag.

"Somebody accidentally knocked over a candy bar display."

Now the chief glared over at Jamal Wilson. "Was it the black boy?"

"No," said Karpinski.

"You sure? Black boy looks kind of shifty to me."

"I told you—"

"What about the big drooling idiot? The one they call Mongoose."

"Mongo."

"What?"

"My nickname is Mongo, sir."

"Your name will be whatever I tell you it is, son."

Mongo hung his head. "Yes, sir."

Riley had heard enough. "It was me, okay? I bumped into the cardboard thingy and knocked it over. It was an accident."

Happiness filled Chief Brown's face. He looked like he had just eaten six meatball hoagies and seven bags of chips. "Son, there is no such thing as an accident when a known troublemaker such as yourself is on the loose. Let's go. You're coming with me."

"What?"

The chief laid his big whopping hand on Riley's shoulder and squeezed hard. "Congratulations, Riley Mack. You just won yourself a free ride in the backseat of my police car."

JENNY GRABOWSKI WATCHED THE POLICE car cruise up
Main Street with its roof lights swirling.

Judging by the silhouettes she saw inside the car, the
driver was a bloated beach ball of a man, his stomach
seemingly attached at the belly button to the steering
wheel. The criminal, seated calmly in the backseat,
appeared to be very short, with a crown of shaggy
hair. Jenny shook her head and hoped the big man
hadn't hurt the little one, the way big humans so often
hurt smaller creatures.

Jenny Grabowski had just turned twenty-two and had
a soft spot for weak and innocent creatures. That's why
she loved her new job at Mr. Guy's Pet Supplies, the

shop directly across the street from the First National Bank of Fairview. Truth be told, she thought cats and dogs, guinea pigs and parakeets were sometimes better company than people.

Before she started working at Mr. Guy's, Jenny had volunteered at the Humane Society's animal shelter, where the veterinarians had encouraged Jenny to apply for vet school in the fall. Jenny already had three cats at home, walked her neighbors' dogs for them whenever they went on vacation, and always carried bread crumbs in her pockets to feed the pigeons over in Sherman Green Park. And she never stepped on ants.

Her boyfriend, Andrew, was an even bigger animal nut. He'd once strapped himself to a supermarket lobster tank with bicycle chains, demanding that the fish department "Free the crustaceans!" Now Andrew worked as an airport limousine driver to pay off his legal bills.

Mr. Guy's Pet Supplies didn't sell pets. No puppies, kittens, bunnies, birdies, or turtles. Just supplies. But Jenny had arranged for the animal shelter to showcase almost a half dozen of the Humane Society's adoptable dogs in the store.

The bell harness hanging over the front door jingled and all the rescues up for adoption started barking and yapping.

"Hello!" Jenny called out to the squat woman who trundled into the store. "May I help you?"

"Who are you?"

"Jenny."

"You're new."

"Yes, ma'am," said Jenny, barely able to contain her joy. "This is my first week!"

"Need dog food," the woman said brusquely. "Big bag."

"Sure. What kind?"

"Cheapest you got. None of that fancy-schmancy stuff with carrots and crap." The woman's scowling face was wrapped up tight in a red-checkered scarf tied snugly under her chin. She appeared to be sixty, maybe seventy. She also smelled like poop.

Yes! The heavenly, yet earthy, aroma of animal dung, Jenny's favorite scent. She wished they made barnyard poop perfume! She'd wear it every day. So would Andrew.

Jenny glanced down at the woman's rubber work boots peeking out under the hem of her ankle-length skirt. They were speckled with mud and muck.

"Do you live on a farm, ma'am?" Jenny asked, her voice filled with admiration.

"Get out of my way, missy." The old woman plowed up the aisle toward the brightly colored sacks of kibble. "Need a seventy-pound bag and someone to haul it out to my truck."

"Well, we have many fine brands to choose from."

"I told you—I want the cheap chow."

One of the adoptable dogs in the nearby crates grumbled.

"Ah, shut up!" The old woman smacked the side of its cage. Hard. The dog tucked in its tail and whimpered.

"Um, I take it you're more of a cat person?"

The old woman ignored Jenny and glowered at a tiny puppy in a newspaper-lined cage. The skinny dog, a Chihuahua-terrier mix, trembled in fear. Then it peed—a big wet lake that slowly spread out across the sports page.

"What kind of dog is that?" the old woman asked.

"A bitzer."

"Bitzer? What's a bitzer?"

"A mutt," Jenny said with a smile. "You know, a bit of this, a bit of that. A bitzer?"

"That supposed to be funny?"

"Um . . ."

"Mr. Guy never sold dogs in here before."

"Oh, they're not for sale. They're up for adoption."

"Adoption? That's un-American."

"They're from the Humane Society's animal shelter."

"So? You people trying to put dog breeders out of business?"

"No, we're just trying to help these poor, defenseless creatures find homes."

"Defenseless? You ever have a dog bite you in the butt, missy?"

"No . . ."

"That's why these dogs were kicked out of their homes. They're all butt biters. That fanny snapper in the bottom cage is starin' at your derriere right now! So grab that feed sack and be quick about it!"

"Yes, ma'am."

Jenny dragged the seventy-pound bag over to the cash register.

"Will there be anything else today?" she asked, because Mr. Guy, her boss, had trained her to say that every time she checked out a customer, even one as sour as this angry old grump.

"What do you mean, 'anything else'?"

"Well, um, we have a wide selection of dog toys."

"Toys? Ha! Next, you'll be trying to sell me little doggy jackets and doggy sweaters."

Jenny hoped the crabby old prune didn't see the nearby display racks filled with doggy jackets, doggy sweaters, and, yes, doggy boots.

"That'll be twenty dollars," she said nervously. "For the dog food."

"I know what I bought, little Miss Missy Miss." The old lady paid with nineteen wrinkled one-dollar bills, three quarters, two dimes, and a nickel, muttering, "Twenty dollars. Stupid dogs. Eating me out of house and home."

Yes, Jenny liked dogs and cats better than most humans.

This lady?

Jenny liked lizards, snakes, and slugs better than her.

RILEY MACK HAD BEEN HAULED down to police head-quarters a few times before, so he knew how to find the drink machine and where they hid the cookies.

Of course Chief Brown had told him to wait "right here in the holding area, son," which was basically an empty cinderblock room with no windows, a table, a couple chairs, and a stack of wrinkled magazines—not to mention stinky shag carpet, the color of lima beans. Riley wondered if he'd die of mildew poisoning before his mom showed up to spring him free, but he was keeping his cool and would do as he was told.

He had already bopped down the hall, bought himself a nice cold soda, and snagged a couple chocolate chip cookies out of the secret snack cabinet.

Drink finished, cookie crumbs dusted off his pants, he checked out the magazine lying on the top of the heap of tired old reading material. The cover showed a U.S. Army Special Forces commando with long hair and a bushy red beard. Goggles up, he was casually corralling a pack of enemy combatants, holding his rifle tight but easy against his chest. The guy looked like a pirate, with a camo bandanna and a daring glint in his eyes.

It wasn't Riley's dad, but it could have been.

His father, Colonel Richard Mack, who everybody called Mack, was currently stationed with the Special Forces over in Afghanistan, just outside Jalalabad—pretty close to the Pakistan border. Thanks to internet videoconferencing technology, Riley and his dad talked most nights—chatting across several thousand miles and a half day's worth of time zones.

They'd definitely be talking tonight.

Riley's mom would make sure of that.

Unless, of course, his dad was off doing something more dangerous than dealing with a high school freshman who liked to pick on fifth graders.

"All the bad guys aren't over here, Riley," his dad once told him. "Protect your country, protect your family, protect your friends, and defend those who cannot defend themselves. And, while you're doing it, try to enjoy the ride."

Yeah. Riley thought his dad was awesome.

The first time Riley had been hauled to the police building was the only time he'd actually deserved it. A couple days before his ninth birthday, his father received new orders and shipped out to a far-off combat zone. That meant he wouldn't be around to celebrate Riley's big day with ice cream and cake.

First, that made Riley sad. Next, it made him mad. Then, he did something extremely bad.

On the morning of his ninth birthday, Riley went to the supermarket and stole a whole ice-cream cake, which he stuffed down the front of his pants. Riley had always been clever. Cunning. But that day, he was actually kind of stupid.

First of all, an ice-cream cake is a pretty huge thing to smuggle out of a store inside your pants. Second, the ice cream melted quickly, so wherever Riley walked, he dribbled an easy-to-follow trail of sticky goo. He was busted before he made it past the baggers.

He and his dad had a long, long talk on their laptops that night.

Surprisingly, his father didn't yell or scream. Didn't threaten to have Riley's mom take away all his video games or lock him in his room till he turned eighteen. In fact, his father remained eerily calm.

"Son," he said, his voice coming out of the computer

speakers strong and firm, "as you know, I cannot be there to babysit you twenty-four seven. Therefore, you have a choice. You can keep acting up, being selfish, causing your mother grief. Or you can use your incredible skills and talents to serve something bigger than yourself. Your choice, son. I suggest you choose wisely."

The door opened.

His mom came into the holding room.

"Okay, kiddo. What happened this time?"

Riley shrugged. "Nothing."

"Nothing? Riley, the chief of police said you were shoplifting again."

"The chief of police has a very vivid imagination."

His mom sank down into a chair with a heavy sigh. "Riley? Come on. This isn't funny."

"I'm telling you the truth. Honest. Just ask Mr. Karpinski. He's the manager at the Quick Pick."

"Did you threaten to send Mongo after his family?"

"No. Mongo was already with me. Jake and Briana, too."

Another sigh. This one shot sideways out of her mouth. It sent her copper curls bouncing.

"Why were you guys at the Quick Pick instead of the Pizza Palace doing your homework?"

"The police chief's son, Gavin Brown, was over there picking on this fifth grader."

"Gavin? I thought he graduated from middle school."

"He did. And only a year or two later than he was supposed to."

"So what's he doing coming back to pick on fifth graders?"

"A lot of fifth graders won't fight back. Most high school kids, on the other hand, will. When we got to the Quick Pick, Gavin had this little dude's head jammed into the frozen food case at the back of the store. He was giving the kid what they call a 'freezy wheezy.' So we ran a little scam that convinced Gavin to act otherwise."

"Freezy wheezy? Is that like a wedgie?"

"No. It's brand-new. I think Gavin invented it."

His mom released sigh number three.

"Look, hon—Gavin Brown is a big, bullying baby who always goes running to his daddy every time you outfox him. Then the chief trumps up some kind of excuse to haul your butt down here so I have to haul my butt out of work. . . ."

"Sorry, Mom."

"Well, it's not your fault. Completely. Just promise me you'll stay away from this boy, okay?"

"Okay. Unless, of course, Gavin brings the fight to me, my friends, or another innocent kid. I can't just look the other way."

"Maybe you should, Ri."

"Mom, Dad always says, 'Never run away from danger. Never, never, never. If you do, you only double that danger.'"

"He says that, huh? All those *never*s?"

"Yeah. But I think Winston Churchill said it first."

A smile quivered across his mom's lips. "He's a smart man, your pops. I miss him, you know? I miss him bad."

"Me, too," said Riley. "But don't worry, Mom. We're gonna be okay. I've got your back."

That made her laugh. "Oh you do, do you?"

"Yes, ma'am."

They were both smiling now.

"Come on," said his mom, standing up. "Let's get you home. Oh, if Chief Brown asks, you're grounded for the next fifteen years."

"Really?"

"For defending an innocent kid from an overgrown goon? Uh, no—I don't think so."

That's when the door swung open. Chief Brown strode into the cramped room.

Riley pretended to pout. "Aw, Mom. No TV and no computer for a month?"

"You heard me, Riley Mack."

"But, Mom?" he whined. Briana had taught him how to make it sound legit.

"You want to try for two months?"

"No . . ."

"I take it you two had that little talk, Mrs. Mack?" said the chief, a sneer curling his lip up toward his nose. He had a flat flounder face, too. Like father, like son.

"Yes, chief," said Riley's mom. "He's very sorry."

The chief faked a cheesy smile. "Mrs. Mack, I know your husband is away, serving his country overseas. Everybody tells me he's some kind of hero."

Riley's mom narrowed her eyes. "And?"

"Well, don't you think you and your son might be happier living out on the army base instead of here in town?"

"We have family here."

"Still. Might be best for everyone if you two left town."

"Why, Chief Brown, is that a threat?"

"No, ma'am. Just a friendly suggestion."

"Well, then, I have a friendly suggestion for you."

"Excuse me?"

"Tonight, for dessert, ask your son to give you a freezy wheezy. From what I hear, they're delicious."

MRS. MACK'S BOSS, CHUCK "CALL me Chip" Weitzel, had dreamed of being a banker ever since he was a young boy cheating at Monopoly.

Whenever he played, he volunteered to be the banker because that put him in charge of the box lid with all the make-believe money stacked inside. It was *so* easy to slip yourself an extra one-hundred-dollar bill every time you passed Go, to pocket a few Beauty Taxes. You could even grab a bright green house and plop it down on your best property while everybody else was crawling around on the floor searching for the metal shoe you accidentally knocked off Marvin Gardens.

Being a banker was why he flew to Las Vegas once a

month for investment opportunities.

"Welcome back, Mr. Weitzel," said the valet-parking attendant.

"Welcome back, Mr. Weitzel," said the bellman and the hotel clerk and the maids and the heavyweight champion boxer the casino paid to say hello to people in the lobby.

"Welcome back, sir," said the woman in the tuxedo shirt and red bow tie who spun the roulette wheel on the casino floor.

Mr. Weitzel had been going to Las Vegas on a regular basis for about a year to make his money grow. He didn't overdo it, of course. That wouldn't be prudent and, as everybody knows, bankers are extremely prudent and conservative. They have to be or other people, total strangers, wouldn't trust them with all their money. So Chuck Weitzel only flew out to Las Vegas once a month for a weekend of what he called "unrivaled investment opportunities"—what other people, cynical people, called "gambling."

"Chips for Chip," he said, sliding a mountain of cash across the green felt.

"Fifties?" the dealer asked, pointing to her colorful assortment of poker chips.

"Make them hundreds."

"Here you go, sir." The dealer pushed ten neatly stacked towers of ten black chips each across the table.

"Ten thousand dollars."

As he leaned down to scoop up his stakes, the banker felt something stiff rub against his chest.

Whoops. He had forgotten that he had another envelope of cash stuffed inside his suit coat.

He pulled it out.

Funny. The money smelled like coffee beans.

He figured Mrs. Rollison must have kept her two thousand dollars stashed in a coffee can before she brought it to Mrs. Mack's window at the bank yesterday afternoon.

Mr. Weitzel smiled and asked for more chips.

"Another two thousand."

If pressed, the senile Mrs. Rollison would most likely say she had given her two thousand dollars to her favorite bank teller, sweet Mrs. Madiera Mack at window three.

That made the banker's smile grow even broader.

There was a very good reason why he always offered to take over Mrs. Mack's window on the Friday afternoons before his monthly investment trips to Las Vegas.

If anything bad happens to the bank's money, folks would know exactly who to blame!

And it wouldn't be Chuck "call me Chip" Weitzel.

THE NEXT WEEK AT SCHOOL, adoring fifth graders mobbed Riley Mack.

They followed him up the hall, patted him on the back, asked for his autograph, and offered him the potato chips from their lunch sacks. It was like having a fan club. Some of the fifth grade girls gave Riley frilly Valentine's Day cards even though February 14 had passed, like, three months earlier.

The new kid, Jamal Wilson—who, it turned out, was very verbose (one of the words he had memorized from the *V* section of the dictionary) when his face wasn't stuffed inside the deep freeze—had told every kid in the fifth grade the details of what had gone down at the Quick Pick Mini Mart, including the chief's new nickname for Riley and his gang—the Gnat Pack.

It sort of stuck and Riley didn't mind.

Gnats were tiny menaces, clever little pests with the power to drive grown-ups—who weighed maybe five kajillion times more than the itty-bitty bugs—crazy.

Riley's dad was proud of him, too.

"You did the right thing, Riley," he said when they linked up on their laptops. "Keep up the good work, son."

"Thanks. But Mom says I should stay away from Gavin Brown for a while, on account of the fact that his dad is the chief of police and all."

His father's face turned super serious while he contemplated that. "Can you do as your mother has requested, son?"

"Sure. If, you know, Gavin has learned his lesson."

"I'll bet he has. Bullies are always cowards at heart. And a coward is one who, in a perilous situation, always thinks with his legs."

Riley chuckled.

"So let's call off any further Brown intervention," his father continued. "Of all the stratagems ever devised, to know when to quit is the best."

"Did Winston Churchill say that?"

In the grainy window on his computer screen, Riley could see his dad smiling as he shook his head.

"Negative. It's an old Chinese proverb. I believe I first read it in a fortune cookie."

"Cool." Riley hoped his dad could see his smile, too.

"Let's avoid Gavin Brown with extreme prejudice. Your mom has enough on her plate right now."

"Yes, sir."

"Promise?"

"Yeah."

"Good. Because I have to go dark for about a week. My men and I are moving out."

"Where to?"

"That information is classified. If I told you, I'd have to shoot you. And son?"

"Sir?"

"I love you far too much to have to do that."

"Yes, sir."

Riley gave his dad a two-finger salute. His dad gave him one right back. And then they talked about baseball and other junk for over an hour.

Friday morning at school, one week after the Quick Pick Caper, Jamal Wilson was all of a sudden at the locker right next to Riley's, tugging down hard on the shackle of the combination lock and slowly turning the dial clockwise.

"Good morning, Riley Mack."

Riley nodded. "Jamal."

"Hey, do you know what people are saying about you and your friends?" Jamal clicked the lock's dial two more ticks then cranked it counterclockwise.

"I've heard a few things."

"You and Mongo and Jake and Briana are illustrious. You know what that word means?"

Riley shrugged because he knew Jamal would tell him.

"Means y'all are renowned, which is another word for eminent, esteemed, or extolled."

"You spent some time in the *E* section of the dictionary?"

"Last night. I was hoping to find the exact words to express my gratitude and appreciation for what you and your crew did for me last Friday." While Jamal said all that, he had reversed course on the combination lock and was clicking the dial hard to the right again while still tugging down on the U-shaped hasp. The lock made choppy noises as he forced it forward.

"Got it," said Jamal. The lock popped open.

"That your locker now?" Riley asked.

"Nah." He opened the door. "My locker's over with the fifth graders."

"So how come you know the combination?"

"I don't. I just like to fidget with things. Figure out what makes them tick. You ever play with a Rubik's Cube?"

"Once," said Riley. "I got bored."

"I hear you talking, Riley Mack. I mean, once you twist it and turn it and waste a whole minute making all the squares the same color on each side, what are you supposed to do with that thing, use it as a paper-weight?"

Riley was impressed. "So how did you open that lock?"

"Oh, I'm a fan of lock sports."

"And what, exactly, are those?"

"An amateur association of puzzle solvers on the web. We swap tricks on how to pick locks. We do it as a divertissement or beguilement. You know what those words mean?"

"Yeah. You stay out of jail because you don't actually crack open any locks."

Jamal closed the locker next to Riley's. "Well, sometimes we do. But we always lock 'em back up afterward."

"So how'd you figure out the combination?"

"Simple. You just have to know how to feel out the numbers. Of course, the first number isn't the first click you feel. It's two past the first click. That's really the only tricky thing you need to remember."

"Is that so?"

"Yeah. Takes me twelve seconds to crack open a standard combination lock."

"Interesting."

"I'm also very good at mechanical, dexterity, pattern, and sequential movement puzzles. Perhaps y'all could utilize a self-taught and extremely ingenious individual such as myself?"

"For what?"

"Your next caper! We gotta get our stuff back!"

"What stuff?"

"That butt head Brown stole two of my iPods, man! And, I can prove which ones are mine on account of the fact that I had 'This is mine, Jamal Wilson' and 'This is mine, too, Jamal Wilson' engraved on the backs of 'em."

"Why did you have two iPods?"

"In case I lost one, which I did!"

"Look, Jamal—I'm sorry for your loss."

"This isn't all about me." Jamal pulled a folded-over sheet of notebook paper out of his pocket. "This is a list of all the other items Gavin Brown has stolen from all the other fifth graders. Just look at it!"

Riley did.

It was a very long list: an MP3 recording karaoke player, several Nintendo DS Lites, assorted iPods, something called a chunky lucky charm bracelet, a robot, baseball mitts, pendant cameras, talking key chains, neoprene lunch totes, a kickboard scooter, Swatch watches, boom boxes, a ten-karat-gold cupcake necklace, a Nerf dart blaster, wallets, coin purses—on and on.

The itemized inventory filled the entire front and back of the sheet of paper.

"A Lava Lamp?" said Riley.

Jamal nodded. "Girl named Kayla was bringing it in for show-and-tell." He shrugged. "Girls. Am I right, Riley Mack?"

Riley didn't respond. He folded up the paper, handed it back to Jamal, who was staring up at him with big, hopeful eyes.

"Look, Jamal, I like the fact you're speaking up for all the other fifth graders. But, I'm sorry. The Gnat Pack needs to lie low for a while. Stay off the police department's radar. Let's just hope Gavin Brown learned his lesson and leaves you kids alone. I gotta run. See you 'round."

He gave the younger kid a wink and a jaunty two-finger salute off the tip of his eyebrow.

Jamal put his tiny hands on his tiny hips. "That's it?"

"Excuse me?"

"You blowin' me off with a hearty 'buh-bye' and a flip of your fingers?"

"I didn't flip you—"

"I thought you were Riley Mack, man!"

"Look, Jamal . . ."

"Maybe you just *look* like Riley Mack, because the

Riley Mack I met last week, let me tell you: that dude would do whatever it took to see that justice was served and that this long list of wrongs was rectified. You know what *rectified* means? Means you take those wrongs and you make them right! You rectify them!"

"I gotta go."

"You're lettin' down a whole lot of people, man. Some of them Valentine cards people sent you? They were homemade, man. The cookies, too!"

Riley slumped his shoulders and headed up the corridor. He almost turned around and said, *I can't help you, Jamal, because I promised my mom and dad I'd stay away from Gavin Brown.*

But he knew that would only make him sound lamer.

THAT SAME AFTERNOON, CHUCK "CALL me Chip" Weitzel sat in his office at the bank crunching numbers.

Last weekend's trip to Las Vegas had been the best ever. According to the little ledger he kept locked in his desk, he was currently up fifty thousand dollars for the first five months of the year. His revolutionary investment scheme was working. He could buy a new car. Heck, he could buy a couple new cars.

But he wouldn't.

New cars would make people start asking questions.

So instead of tooling around town in a flashy two-seater Corvette convertible, Chuck kept his cash wrapped in neat bundles, locked up tight inside his

FireKing Executive Safe, currently nestled in the bottom drawer (also locked) of his big mahogany desk. As advertised, its handy-dandy mounting system "allowed the compact but incredibly tough safe to be easily moved from desk drawer to car trunk to airplane" headed for Bermuda. Or Jamaica. Maybe Mexico. Someplace where it never snowed and you could drink umbrella drinks all day long and never pay taxes.

Of course, the two thousand dollars Mrs. Rollison had wanted deposited in her passbook savings account last Friday was properly credited to her account first thing Monday morning. For the checks in Mrs. Mack's teller drawer, he just took a "cash advance" from the vault, knowing the money would be returned before the start of the business week (he usually swung by the bank on his way home from the airport on the Sunday night of his Vegas weekends).

Mr. Weitzel leaned back in his padded leather chair and put his feet up on the wooden deck of his boat-sized desk. He wished he could suspend the bank's no-smoking policy and fire up a big fat cigar; then he'd look just like Uncle Pennybags from Monopoly—the guy on the old Chance card that said, "Bank Pays You Dividend of $50."

Yep, when you were the banker, life was a winning game. You took your Chance cards. You made your money.

Chuck Weitzel didn't have a care in the world.

His eyes drifted over to the computer screen on top of his desk. All the bank's security cameras fed into his office, where the digital images were recorded and stored on the hard drive of his computer. Through the matrix of windows on his screen, he could keep his eyes on the ATMs, the lobby, the vault room, the drive-up window, the tellers in their brass cages. Everything.

Including a shaggy-haired, redheaded boy walking across the lobby.

Apparently, Mrs. Mack thought today was "bring your troublemaker son to work" day.

RILEY SKIPPED THE PIZZA PALACE after school.

The rest of his gang had gone over to Mongo's house to check out Noodle, the goldendoodle, which Riley thought sounded like a new kind of cheese curl.

"It's a man-made dog," Jake had explained. "Part golden retriever, part poodle."

"So why didn't they call it a golden poodle?" asked Briana.

"Probably because it would sound too much like a Chinese restaurant," said Riley. "And trust me—you do not want to know what the Golden Poodle puts in its secret recipes."

Jake did a quick Google search on his smartphone

and let everybody know that "goldendoodles were first bred in North America as a larger version of the popular cockapoo. Their nonshedding coats make them very appealing for families with allergies."

Mongo's little sister was allergic to everything. Cats. Dogs. Peanuts. Her big brother's socks. Well, those things made everybody gag and sneeze.

So while the Gnat Pack headed over to the Montgomery house on their bikes to meet the fifteen-hundred-dollar dog, Riley pedaled to the bank to see his mom. He was hoping he could convince her to lift the ban on all actions against Gavin Brown because Riley really wanted to do what Jamal had suggested: he wanted to retrieve all the merchandise the bully had stolen from all those fifth graders.

First, it was the right thing to do.

And second, Riley did not enjoy feeling the way his chat with Jamal Wilson had left him feeling. He didn't like letting people down. "Protect your country, protect your family, protect your friends, and defend those who cannot defend themselves" was what his dad always told him. Well, right now, Riley wasn't doing any of those things. He was lying low and keeping his nose clean. It just wasn't who he was. He was a doer, not a lying-lower.

Riley Mack didn't feel like *Riley Mack* anymore.

In fact, he hadn't felt like such a big-time disappointment since he turned nine and stuffed an ice-cream cake into his underpants.

Since Friday was payday for a lot of people in Fairview, the bank lobby was extremely crowded. Long lines snaked across the marble floor as Riley rolled through the revolving brass door. He went to the back of the line for teller window three, figuring he had to wait his turn to see his mom, which would also give him time to perfect his pitch.

But, being a mom, Riley's mother sixth-sensed his presence the instant he entered the building and motioned for Riley to come up to her window right away.

Riley ducked his head, mumbled, "Excuse me" about a hundred times, and, basically, cut to the front of the line. He heard a bunch of grumbling from the grown-ups he passed, the people he was making wait even longer than they already knew they'd have to wait.

"Riley?" his mom asked when he made it to her window. "Is everything okay, hon?"

"Yeah. I just needed to talk to you."

"Is it urgent?"

"Kind of."

"Can it wait?"

Riley heard a soft whirr come from somewhere up near the ceiling. He glanced to his right and saw a spy camera aimed straight at his mother's teller window.

The lens rotated as it zoomed in for a tighter shot.

Great. Now he was getting his mom in trouble. What a day. He was disappointing everybody, especially himself.

"Riley? I don't have a whole lot of time. I really need to take care of my customers. What's wrong?"

"It's nothing."

"Nothing?"

"Yeah. I just, you know, thought I'd drop by."

"On Friday? During rush hour?"

"Yeah."

His mom did not look pleased.

Neither did the man who suddenly appeared behind her in the teller cage. It was her boss, the bank manager, Mr. Weitzel, the guy named Chuck who, for some bizarro reason, wanted everybody, even Riley, to call him Chip. Mr. Weitzel was glaring at Riley.

"Riley?" his mother said again. "We're kind of busy right now."

"Riiight. Never mind. I needed some money for pizza but I just remembered that Mongo owes me five bucks so I'll get it from him. See you at home." He waved at the scowling man looming behind his mom. "So long, Mr. Weitzel—I mean, Chip."

He pivoted, bolted across the lobby, and spun through the revolving door like he was riding a playground merry-go-round. He came flying out the other side and slid across a pile of dog mess somebody forgot to pooper-scoop off the sidewalk.

Yep, just when Riley didn't think he could feel any lamer, he did. He was a total lame-o. The lame-inator.

He swiped his sneaker clean on the curb, unlocked his bike from a streetlamp, and was about to ride home so he could stick his head inside a brown paper bag and hide his lameosity, when his cell phone started buzzing.

It was Jake.

"Riley, we have an emergency."

"What's up?"

"Noodle is gone."

"The goldendoodle?"

"Yeah. Somebody stole her. Mongo's little sister says it was a Martian."

MONGO HUGGED HIS MOM AND patted her on the back.

She was about a foot shorter than him.

"C'mon, Mom. Don't cry."

Mongo's mom kept crying, burrowing her face in her enormous son's equally enormous armpit, which muffled her sobs and must've smelled pretty bad, too.

Riley was hanging out with Mongo's sister, six-year-old Emma, who was rocking in a wicker chair up on the porch while her mother and big brother hugged it out on the steps. Briana and Jake were down on the lawn, looking up at Riley. Riley gave them the "hang on a second" hand signal.

"So, Emma," he said, "what's this about a Martian?"

"A space alien hopped over the fence and grabbed Noodle and put her in his rocket ship and blasted off."

"Is that so?"

"Uh-huh. It sounded like this!" Emma puckered up her lips and blew. Riley got a faceful of spittle. Emma's sound effects were the same as the motorboat noises one might accidentally make in the bathtub after eating too many baked beans.

"This space creature," Riley asked next. "What'd it look like?"

"He had Ping-Pong ball eyes the size of hard-boiled eggs!" said Emma.

"Uh-huh."

"His skin was green."

"Huh."

"His head was this tall!"

She held her hand higher than Abe Lincoln's top hat.

"And, and, and—he had two stumps where someone cut off his antlers."

"Oh-kay. Big eyes. Big head. Antlers."

"But the antlers were chopped off!"

"Right. Thanks, Emma."

Riley turned to his friends on the lawn. Rolled his eyes. Mongo's little sister seemed just a wee bit wacked.

"Come inside, Emma!" said Mongo's mom. "I need to call the police. You need to tell them what happened."

"You mean the Martian?"

"No—how you forgot to close the gate in the back-yard and Noodle ran away."

"But that's not what happened! The spaceman took Noodle to his spaceship."

She started in with the lip-fart noises again.

Mrs. Montgomery scooted Emma into the house. Mongo and Riley came down the steps to join Briana and Jake in the yard.

"We need to check out the backyard," said Riley. "See what's what."

Mongo led the way around the house.

"What'd your mom say?" Riley asked him.

"Emma was in the back having a tea party with the puppy and a couple of my teddy bears. She left the gate open. Noodle made a break for it."

"When'd this happen?"

"Right before we got here," said Jake. "Maybe fifteen minutes ago."

They reached the backyard. Saw the plastic teakettle and cups. The open gate in the fence.

"Okay," said Riley. "We need to make a poster. Fly-ers. I want Noodle's face on every telephone pole and parking meter in town."

"We should offer a reward," said Jake.

Briana gasped. "Wait, you guys! What if some sicko *stole* the puppy precisely because they knew there'd be a reward!"

"The thought had crossed my mind," said Riley. "Emma's alien could've been a dognapper in a Halloween Martian mask."

"I'll kill him!" said Mongo, his whole body seizing up with rage, the way it used to back in fifth grade when kids made fun of his backpack bears.

"I imagine you will," said Riley. "But, first, let's get your dog back."

"Then can I kill the creep?"

Riley patted his friend's ribs. He couldn't reach his shoulder. "We'll talk."

"Should I close the gate?" asked Jake.

"Let's leave it open," said Riley. "There's always a chance Noodle will sniff her way home."

They returned to the front of the house. Mrs. Montgomery was on the porch, screaming at the telephone clenched in her fist.

"Too busy? Well, you tell Chief Brown that maybe next time he is raising money for the Fairview Police Benevolence Fund we'll be too busy to contribute!" She yanked the phone away from her ear as if it had stung her. "They hung up on me!"

"Mrs. Montgomery?" said Riley. "Jake here is going to put together some flyers. We need to know: Is there a reward?"

"Yes."

"How much, Mom?" asked Mongo.

"I don't know. What do you think, Riley?"

"Well, I don't think we need to name a number. A big one might motivate the wrong sort of people, if you catch my drift."

"Riley's right!" said Briana—very dramatically, of course. "Dognappers! Pooch pinchers! Beagle burglars!"

Now Riley gave Briana the "cut" sign and smiled up at Mrs. Montgomery. "We'll just say 'reward' and list your phone number."

"Check," said Jake, who was taking notes.

"And Jake? No names. Just Mrs. M's phone number."

"Gotcha!"

"Mrs. Montgomery," said Riley, "can you give us any distinguishing characteristics for Noodle? Something that might make her easier to spot?"

"Well, she has golden, curly hair. Big soft eyes."

"And a wet teddy bear nose," added Mongo.

"Anything more specific?" asked Riley.

"Does she have any tattoos?" said Jake, who watched way too many *CSI* shows on TV.

"No, but she was wearing her pink collar," said Mrs. Montgomery. "The one in the photograph I showed you kids."

"The one with all the bling?" asked Briana.

"The what?"

"Sparkly things," said Riley.

71

"You know," said Briana. "*Bling-bling.* That's the sound a sparkle makes in a toothpaste commercial."

"I see," said Mongo's mom. "Yes, she was wearing her jeweled collar."

"Make that *fake* jeweled collar," Riley said to Jake. "Real jewels might also draw the interest of the wrong individuals."

"Got it," said Jake.

"Okay, people," said Riley. "We need to move quickly if we want to stay ahead of the dog. Alert your parental units. Could be a long night. I recommend we cover a three-mile radius moving out from this point. We don't get any hits, we call up more troops, cover a wider area. Tomorrow morning, we go door to door if we have to. Mrs. Montgomery?"

"Yes, Riley?"

"Before you take off in your car and search for Noodle . . ."

"How did you know . . ."

"It's your next logical move, ma'am. But, before you do, I suggest you call the folks at the Fairview Humane Society's animal shelter. It's possible somebody found Noodle and took her to the shelter. I'm guessing she doesn't have her tags yet?"

"That's right. I only picked her up last week. I haven't had time. . . ."

"Understandable," said Riley calmly, because he

didn't want Mrs. Montgomery to feel as bad as *he* had when Jamal Wilson pointed out how he was letting everybody down.

"We called her Noodle," said Mongo, "because it rhymes. With *doodle*."

Riley nodded. It was pretty clear that even though Noodle had only been with the Montgomery family for a little over a week, she had already stolen their hearts.

Mrs. Montgomery called the animal shelter, and then she and Emma took off in the car.

Riley and his crew went to Jake's house, put together the poster, and printed it up.

Then they spread out. Canvassed the town.

When Riley's mom got off work, she helped, too. So did Jake's and Briana's parents.

By eleven p.m., every utility pole, parking meter, and shop window in Fairview was covered.

At midnight, Riley finally went to bed, totally frustrated.

Noodle was still missing. Not one person had seen the puppy or her flashy pink collar.

That all changed first thing Saturday morning.

AT 9:01 A.M. ON SATURDAY, Jamal Wilson sent Riley Mack an urgent text message with a photo attached.

Riley called Jamal back at 9:02 a.m.

"Where are you?"

"The flea market in Sherman Green," Jamal whispered back. "Near the gazebo."

"Which booth?"

"The sign says Grandma's Antiques. You see that Lava Lamp in the picture I sent you, Riley Mack?"

"Yeah."

"She's got my iPods, too, man! Only she messed with the engraving on the back. Says, 'This is mini Jam son' because she scratched out a bunch of the letters in 'This is mine, Jamal Wilson' and changed the *e* in *mine* to an *i*!"

"Hang tight, Jamal. Don't say anything to anybody. This is a whole lot bigger than you think."

"Oh, is that so? Because I think it's colossal, enormous, elephantine!"

"Jamal?"

"Yeah?"

"Chill. I'm on my way."

Riley's mom had to work Saturdays at the bank. That meant he was on his own.

He grabbed his bike—a fire-engine-red Frantic with twenty-inch wheels, aluminum rims, mud flap fenders, and BMX pads—and headed over to Sherman Green, a small park about a half mile from his house on Maple Lane. Every weekend, the town hosted a farmer's market and flea fair. Vendors set up canopied booths and sold everything from goat cheese and apple cider to embroidered blouses and grandfather clocks. The tents on stilts, some with flapping banners and fluttering flags, surrounded a small gazebo in the center of the park, making Sherman Green look like a pop-up Renaissance festival.

Riley chained his bike to a rack and headed into the open-air flea fair. He passed a guy selling sand candles, a lady hawking perfume, and what seemed like a million jewelry tents. As he neared the gazebo, he saw a weedy patch cluttered with crap. Mirrors, baskets, chairs, garden statuary, floor lamps with beaded shades. Behind the price-tagged trash, he saw a sign in frilly froufrou letters:

Grandma's Antiques
One Man's Trash
Is Another Man's Treasure

Make that, "One kid's stolen iPod is another kid's bargain," thought Riley.

Grandma, or whoever was moving the merchandise, had three white tents linked together to cover at least ten cafeteria-sized tables piled high with junk: old tin signs, musty magazines, chipped crockery, an avocado-green coffeemaker, discarded Christmas decorations—a whole landfill's worth of yesterday's garbage.

As Riley moved closer, he saw a nasty old lady with a red-and-white checkered kerchief covering her head. Her nose was the size and shape of a yam. Her baggy cheeks resembled sagging bags of mud. Her eyes were tight black olive pits and her mouth was furrowed in a frown so deep it made her chin look like the one on a ventriloquist's dummy.

She had to be Grandma.

"Pssst! Riley Mack! Over here, man!"

It was Jamal. Hiding behind a rack of handbags in the booth directly across from Grandma's Antiques.

"What took you so long?"

"Had to bike it. My mom's working today."

"My mom dragged me here. She digs the local produce. I ditched her back at the goat yogurt and rutabagas."

"Where'd you snap the shot you sent?" asked Riley.

"In the back of Grandma's tent, man. Over there on the right."

Riley nodded. Over at Grandma's, he saw a man hold up an antique glass bowl to examine it. The old woman slugged him in the arm. This, of course, startled the man, who almost fumbled the bowl but caught it before it crashed.

"You break it, you buy it!" snarled the old woman, right before she spit out some brown, stringy saliva.

"How much?" the man asked when he'd regained his balance.

"If you have to ask"—another chocolaty spit—"you can't afford it."

Gross. She was chewing tobacco.

"I'll give you ten bucks for it."

"Ten bucks?" She snatched the bowl out of the man's

hands. "Beat it, you piker. I sell serious merchandise to serious collectors. You want something for ten bucks, go buy yourself a loaf of banana bread."

"Come on," said Riley. "We need to take a closer look at that table filled with stolen loot."

"It's all there, man!" said Jamal. "Everything on the list. The iPods, Rodman John's robot, Sarah Clare's kickboard scooter."

"I'm interested in the jewelry."

"That's back there, too. Swatch watches, that ten-karat gold cupcake necklace."

"I'm mostly interested in the diamonds."

"Huh?"

"In the picture you sent, I saw what looked like a dog collar."

"Nah. I don't think Gavin Brown stole a fifth grader's dog collar."

"This one is covered with pink bling."

Riley and Jamal entered the tents.

"Don't touch anything, you rug rats," snapped the grumpy old woman. "Where the blazes are your parents?"

"Busy," said Riley, pulling a fifty-dollar bill out of his pocket, flipping it up between his first two fingers. "I'm looking to buy my dog something special for his birthday. Got any dog collars? Maybe something, oh, I don't know—sparkly?"

"You're in luck, Red," said the granny, with another syrupy spit. "Something like that just came in. Check it out. On the back table, there."

"Thanks. Come on, Jimmy."

Riley led the way. Jamal followed.

"Why you callin' me Jimmy?" he whispered. "My name's Jamal. . . ."

"Shhh. The less she knows about who we really are, the better."

"Where'd you get that fifty-dollar bill, man?"

"My grandparents. Two Christmases ago."

"And you haven't spent it yet?"

"Nope. It's my 'flash cash.' Comes in handy."

"So how come she called you Red?"

Riley jabbed a quick thumb up at his hair.

"That ain't red, man. That's orange. Maybe auburn or tawny chestnut. You know what those words mean?"

"Yeah. Red."

They reached the table.

"See? It's all there. What are you gonna do, Riley Mack?"

Riley didn't answer right away. He picked up the pink "diamond" doggy collar and tugged a copy of the Lost Dog flyer out of his jeans.

"Now what're you doing?"

"Making sure."

"Of what?"

"That Gavin Brown has branched out." Yep. The collar on the table was the collar in the photo. "Seems he's not just stealing merchandise from fifth graders these days. He's snatching dogs from kids in kindergarten, too."

"Hey!" shouted the old lady. "Don't play with that. You break it, you bought it."

Riley smiled. He was ready to go back and have a few choice words with the yam-nosed old hag. Ask her who her supplier was. See if the name Gavin Brown rang a bell.

He took one step forward.

Froze.

Chief Brown strode into the tent. He hugged the old woman and kissed her on her wrinkled cheek.

"Good morning, Mom," said the chief. "How's business?"

14

RILEY SAID SO LONG TO Jamal and called an emergency meeting of his crew—in the parking lot of the middle school because the Pizza Palace didn't open till noon on Saturdays.

Yes, he had promised his mom and his dad that he'd stay away from Gavin Brown. But right was right, and wrong was wrong. Stealing a puppy from one of Riley's best buds? That was definitely wrong and needed a little righting.

"In short," said Riley, "we can call off the search party. Gavin Brown stole Noodle. He gave her collar to his grandmother to sell in her junk tent."

"I'm going to hurt Brown so bad!" said Mongo,

slamming his fist into his palm. "His new name will be Black-and-blue!"

"That's the wrong move," said Riley. "If we push Gavin, he'll just deny it, go running to his daddy. If we push too hard, maybe he hurts the dog."

Jake, tucked inside his hoodie, nodded. "It would be in keeping with his sociopathic character."

"But, Riley," whined Briana, "we *have* to do *something*!"

"Don't worry. We will. The Browns are not getting away with this."

"Thank you," said Mongo.

"Now then," said Riley, "I figure there are two ways we can play this thing. One, we do what we've been doing. We keep the posters up; maybe make some new ones where the word *Reward* is bigger, bolder. In a couple days, when they think Mongo's mom is super desperate and willing to pay whatever they ask, someone, probably not Gavin or the chief, but someone working for the Browns will make the call. When they do . . ."

Briana gasped. Shot up her arm. She knew this answer. "We call the police!"

The boys all arched their eyebrows. Stared at her.

"Um, Briana?" said Jake. "Chief Brown *is* the police."

"Oh. Right. *Duh.* My bad."

"When the caller makes contact," said Riley, "we

find out where the money drop is set to take place."

Mongo raised his bicycle up over his head with both hands. Started thrashing it around. "And then we ambush the guy and jump him and kick him and . . ."

Mongo only stopped because Riley was shaking his head.

"We don't do that?" Mongo said, gently lowering the bike.

"No," said Riley. "You give him the cash and take your dog home."

"That's it?"

"Yep. That's all *you* do. Meanwhile, Jake, Briana, and I video the whole transaction. We tail the dognapper. We follow the money all the way back to Brown's house, no matter how many stops it makes along the way or how many couriers relay it back to poppa. When we have proof, we take it to some friends of my father's, former soldiers now employed by the FBI."

"Why don't we just call those guys right now?" said Jake.

"Right. Dognapping. I believe it is currently at the top of the FBI's priority list, right up there with terrorism and counterfeiting."

"Got it," said Jake. "We wait. Till we have solid proof."

Mongo's eyes widened in anticipation. "So what's the second option?"

Riley smiled and pulled a sheaf of paper out of his jeans jacket. He had another devilish gleam in his eyes. "The second option is a little more complicated. A little more fun. A little more what we do best."

"Fabtastic!" said Briana. "Spill."

Riley passed around the stack of papers. "I just worked this up. Ran off a couple copies at the drugstore. I call it Operation Blind Date."

"Nice," said Jake.

"I likee, I likee," added Briana.

"What do we do?" asked Mongo.

"We convince Gavin to give our friend Briana here a certain goldendoodle."

"We do?" said Briana. "How?"

"Gavin won't know it's *you* he's giving it to. Now, to get this ball rolling, we need to case the high school. This afternoon. There's a big baseball game. Crosstown rivals. Fairview versus Western Prep. Jake?"

"Yeah?"

"We need to get Mongo into the stands."

"No problem. I'll dummy up a ticket with a legit bar code."

"Good. Mongo, you're in the cheering section. Up with the freshmen. We give you a little lip fuzz, maybe a dorky Fairview High baseball cap to help you pass as a ninth grader. I want you sitting a couple rows behind Brown."

"Okay. Why?"

"Reconnaissance mission. Briana? You'll work the crowd. I'll line you up a gig selling peanuts and Cracker Jack. Roam the stands. Keep one eye on Gavin Brown, the other eye on whoever he has his eye on."

"Oh-kay," said Briana. "I have this red-and-white striped apron and a paper hat that'll make me look very concessionairey."

"Works for me."

"But how do I get the vendor job?"

"I know this guy who runs the food stand. He owes me a favor ever since I helped him recover his popcorn popper."

"Where was it?"

"You don't want to know. While you two are in the stands, I'll be down on the field with a camera. Jake?"

"You need a press pass?"

"You read my mind. I'll also need your camera. The one with the really long lens."

Jake made a note. "No problem. You sure Brown will be at the game?"

"Positive," said Riley. "Before Jamal and I left the antiques tent, I heard the chief tell Grandma Brown that 'Gavin has the rest of the day off.' Said he was going to 'the big baseball game because he has a crush on one of the cheerleaders.' Granny was cool with that. Said, 'I can't move half the crap he hauls in, anyway.' She wanted more plasma screen TVs, fewer karaoke microphones."

"You want me at the game?" asked Jake.

"No. We need you to babysit Jamal Wilson."

"Come again?"

"He's in on this thing, on account of the stash of fifth-grader swag Grandma's peddling in her pup tent. He can help you on the computer, too."

"I don't know. . . ."

"He's a good kid. Smart. Very manually dexterous. Worked a Rubik's Cube in under a minute."

"No. Way!" said Briana.

"Way. He can also crack locks."

"For real?" said Mongo. "Like in the movies?"

"For real," said Riley.

"Okay. He can hang at my house," said Jake.

"Excellent. Once we dig up the intel, we'll need you guys to find her phone number."

Jake furrowed his brow. "So, um, whose number, exactly, are we looking for again?"

"Whoever this cheerleader is that Gavin Brown has a mad crush on."

"No problem. You tell me her name, I'll tell you her landline, cell, fax, whatever. I can even fish for her email, Twitter, and Facebook pages, too."

"No thanks. All we need is her phone number."

"Um, pardon me for asking, Riley," said Briana, "but, why, all of a sudden, do you want some high school hottie's phone number?"

He smiled at Briana. "So *you* can call her."

THAT SAME SATURDAY MORNING, TWO shady men sat hunkered behind the tinted windows of a battered blue van.

The driver had pulled into the perfect parking spot: directly across the street from the First National Bank of Fairview.

"You see what they're calling us?" said the one in the passenger seat, flipping through the back pages of a tabloid newspaper.

"Yeah," said the driver, who was rolling a toothpick from one side of his lips to the other. "I seen it."

"'The Suburban Buckeye Bandits.'" The man in the

passenger seat angrily wadded up the paper. "I am not buckeyed."

"I know this," said the driver.

"I just have what they call a slight strabismus, on account of the fact that my two eyeballs are not properly aligned with each other. Got a little lack of coordination going on between the extraocular muscles is all."

"Fred?" said the driver.

"Yeah, Otto?" said the passenger.

"Your strabismus there means you're cross-eyed, not buckeyed."

"Oh. That true?"

"Yeah."

"So why's the newspaper calling me a buckeye bandit?"

"On account of the fact we knocked off that string of banks back in Ohio."

"So?"

"Ohio is the Buckeye State."

"They got a lot of cross-eyed people in Ohio?"

"No, Fred. Buckeye is their nickname. On account of the many buckeye trees that once grew there and whatnot."

"Really?"

"Yeah."

"Interesting."

The two men stared at the bank building some more. The driver took the toothpick out of his mouth and grinned.

"Looks like Chuck 'call me Chip' Weitzel isn't as good with security as he is with the roulette wheel," he said.

Now the two shady men both laughed. They had met Mr. Weitzel at a bar in Las Vegas. The banker had extremely minty breath. He had also given Otto and Fred his business card, said he ran "the bestest little bank" in the country. "Stop by sometime when you're back east. We can loan you enough money to get you completely out of debt."

Otto and Fred had both laughed at the bad banker joke. Then they pocketed Mr. Weitzel's business cards and did their homework.

The First National Bank of Fairview—what bank manager Weitzel called "Fin-boff"—was ripe for the picking. Especially on Thursday nights after the branch received its weekly infusion of cash to handle the Friday-afternoon payday rush.

"We do the usual?" asked Fred, staring across the street at Mr. Weitzel's bank.

Otto nodded. "We case the joint for a couple days. Learn how to disarm the alarm."

"Thursday night," said Fred, picking up on Otto's

thread, "when the safe is loaded, we slip on our masks, go in the back door."

"Once we're in the bank, you crack open the safe, I take out the security cameras."

"We load up a few gym bags with moola-boola."

"We waltz out the door."

"We move on to the next sleepy little burb."

Both men sank back in their seats and sighed. They were a well-oiled cash machine—an ATM that only made withdrawals.

AT NOON ON SATURDAY, RILEY Mack's Operation Blind Date was in full swing.

Jake Lowenstein went home to set things up on his computer. Jamal Wilson would join him there in about an hour.

Riley, Briana, and Mongo headed downtown on their bikes.

"We need to buy Mongo a baseball hat," said Briana, who was in charge of everybody's disguises, or costumes as she always called them, even though Riley and Mongo begged her not to. "His buzz cut is a total giveaway. The cap will cover it up."

"I already have a baseball hat," said Mongo, teetering

on his two-wheeler. He was so big and his bike so small, he looked like a clown at the circus. "Man, I wish I had a moped like that busboy Nick. I see him riding his motor scooter around town all the time, delivering pizzas. Looks like fun."

"Totally," said Riley.

"You guys?" said Briana. "We were talking baseball caps?"

"I told you," said Mongo, his knees pumping up toward his nose, "I got one."

"Yankees or Mets?"

"Yankees."

"Well, the Fairview High School team is called the Furriers so you need a Furriers cap. You should have one, too, Riley, since you're playing the high school newspaper photographer. Ooh—you should wear yours backward!"

"Good point," said Riley, as they cruised around the corner onto Main Street. "We'll go to Sports Town. They have all sorts of Furriers junk."

The mascot for the Fairview High Furriers was a buck-toothed beaver wearing a puffy mink coat because the original settlers of Fairview had been fur trappers and traders.

Sports Town was one of a cluster of shops in the commercial blocks of Main Street across the street from the bank where Riley's mom worked. As they started locking up their bikes, they saw the busboy from the Pizza Palace, Nick, come walking out of the local pet supply store toting two birdcages, one pink, and the other baby blue.

"How's it going, Nick?" said Riley.

"Great."

"Cool," said Riley. "You got birds?"

"Huh?"

Riley nodded toward the two portable parakeet palaces.

"Oh. Yeah. Boy and girl."

"I get it," said Mongo. "Blue and pink!"

"Yeah. Hey, Mongo, sorry about your mom's dog, man." Nick gestured to one of the Lost Dog posters stapled to a nearby utility pole. "Bummer, dude. Totally."

"Thanks."

"Well, gotta book."

"You workin' today, Nick?" asked Riley.

"Yeah. But not at the PP until later." (Yes, the Pizza Palace had a very unfortunate nickname.)

Riley arched an eyebrow. "You've got a second job?"

"Yeah."

"Where?"

"Here and there."

"What kind of work?"

"This and that."

In the distance, Riley heard a yappy dog bark.

"Later, dudes," said Nick. He bustled up the sidewalk, holding his arms out wide so the bouncing birdcages didn't ding him in the hips.

"Let's go, you guys," said Briana, leading the way up the sidewalk to Sports Town.

The front door of the pet supplies store swung open. A customer came out hugging a fifty-pound sack of dog food. Five dogs bolted out with him.

"Holy crappola!" a woman shouted inside the store.

The guy with the feed sack spun around and nearly tripped himself up as two dogs darted between his legs and dashed out into the street. One was a big, galumphing guy; the other a little white fur ball.

Two bug-eyed Chihuahuas with wildly curly hair sproinking up on top of their heads ran straight toward Briana.

"Grab the Speedy Gonzaleses," Riley shouted over his shoulder as he and Mongo bounded into the street after the two dogs in the most immediate danger of being mowed down by a minivan. A fifth dog—a black Lab puppy with big floppy feet and long flappy ears—merrily loped down the sidewalk in the opposite direction.

A college-aged girl sprinted out of the pet store.

"Help!" she shouted.

"Go after flopsy-wopsy," said Riley as he corralled the white fluff ball in the middle of the street. "We've got these other guys!" Mongo raised his hands to stop traffic as Riley scooped up the yappy lapdog.

The second escapee had gray fur on his muzzle, a shallow tummy, and bony ribs. He was frantically turning around and around in the middle of the road. He seemed pretty old so Riley crept up slow behind him. A car honked.

Yappy yipped.

The dog squatting in the middle of the road pooped.

The car horn blared again.

"Shut up!" Mongo shouted at the driver. "He needs a moment!"

"Easy, easy," Riley said to the creaky dog finishing up its business on the solid yellow line. Poor guy. He wasn't trying to escape. He was just looking for the bathroom.

"You better clean up after your dog!" huffed a mom behind the wheel of her SUV. She, apparently, didn't like any traffic tie-up caused by unexpected doggy doo. Neither did her daughter. They were both scrunching up their noses and making poopy faces at Riley.

Smiling, still clutching the mop-haired pooch against his chest while bending down to escort the old guy by the collar, Riley gave the mom and daughter his sunniest smile. "I'll be back to clean it up. Just need to go get my pooper-scooper."

"I got these guys!" shouted Briana, who was on the

sidewalk doing some kind of loose-limbed chicken dance, struggling to carry one squirming Chihuahua under each arm.

The girl from the pet store came up the sidewalk cuddling the floppy-eared Lab. The dog was manically licking her face like it was a pork-flavored lollipop. "Thank you, guys, so much!" she said, using her foot to open the door. "Can you help me put them back in their cages?"

"Sure," said Riley.

"How'd they escape?" asked Briana, giggling because the two crazy-eyed Chihuahuas were nuzzling under her arms with their noses.

"I don't know," said the girl. She was wearing a green polo shirt with *Mr. Guy's Pet Supplies* embroidered over the pocket. "I think somebody undid the latches on their cages. Two boys were in the store earlier. They said they wanted to look at hamster tunnels. I think they wanted to monkey around."

"Where do you want these guys?" asked Briana.

"Their crates are all back here. Near the dog food."

"Are they for sale?" asked Riley.

"No. They're free—to a loving home." She slid her frisky puppy into its crate and latched the door shut. "Of course, there's a small adoption fee. A donation to the animal shelter."

"Works for me," said Riley.

"Could these two little guys ride in my purse like they do in Beverly Hills?" asked Briana. "I saw what's-her-name, the movie star, in *People* magazine and she went shopping with two Chihuahuas in her handbag!"

"Would you like to adopt them and find out?" asked the pet shop lady.

"Maybe. I'll have to check with my mom and dad."

"Great. Oh, by the way, I'm Jenny Grabowski. If your folks say yes, just let the store know. Even if I'm not working that day, I'll come in and set up the adoption papers."

"Cool," said Briana, somewhat reluctantly handing off her two wiggly tail waggers.

"I'm Riley Mack," said Riley. "That's Briana Bloomfield and Hubert 'Mongo' Montgomery."

Jenny shook their hands after the last cage was closed. "I can't thank you guys enough for jumping in like that."

Riley shrugged off the compliment. "We see a job that needs doing, we do it."

"And," added Mongo, "we all like dogs."

"Yeah," said Briana. "Especially Amigo and Pepe."

Everybody else looked confused.

"I gave mine names," she explained.

Ms. Grabowski smiled. "You talk it over with your parents, Briana. I'll call my friend Dr. Langston at the

Humane Society, tell her we're holding Amigo and Pepe for you."

"Thanks!"

"Well, we gotta run," said Riley.

"Yeah," said Mongo. "I gotta buy a baseball hat. We need it to find *my* lost dog."

Ms. Grabowski nodded, even though she probably had no idea what Mongo was talking about.

"Thanks again," she said. "And if you ever need any-thing, let me know. I owe you, guys—big-time."

"Thanks," said Riley. "We'll make a mental note."

In fact, as soon as he hit the sidewalk, Riley jotted an entry in the little spiral book he carried to record "favors owed."

He didn't realize how soon he'd be cashing this one in.

ACROSS THE STREET, CHIEF JOHN Brown strode into the First National Bank of Fairview like he owned the place.

Heck, he strode into every place that way. This was his town. He was the law. When he said jump, people said, "How high?" and "Off what bridge, sir?"

Riley Mack's mother was working teller window three. No wonder the boy was such a troublemaker. It was a Saturday, school was out, and here she was at work instead of at home looking after her troublemaking son while her husband was off playing soldier boy over in Afghanistan.

The chief shook his head. Idle hands were the devil's

tools. Kids with nothing to do got into nothing but trouble. That's why John Brown made his boy, Gavin, earn his keep, gave him a monthly quota of "second-hand treasures" to be obtained for his grandmother's antiques tent at the flea market. Kept the boy busy and, at the same time, kept the chief's mom in food and chewing tobacco, which meant Chief Brown didn't have to worry about buying those things for her.

Money, of course, was what brought him to the bank on a Saturday when he was supposed to be out writing up fire code violations for shopkeepers who didn't contribute enough money to his special Police Morale Booster Fund.

"Is Mr. Weitzel available?" he said with a smile to the young woman seated at the customer service desk.

"Is he expecting you?"

"No. But he's going to be very glad to see me. Just tell Chipper that Chief John Brown is here."

"Just a minute, sir." She pressed a button on her phone while the chief hitched up his pants importantly.

"And rustle us up some doughnuts and a fresh pot of coffee." He winked at her before she even answered. "Thanks, doll."

As expected, Chip Weitzel saw Chief Brown right away.

"John! Good to see you!"

They pumped hands.

"You got a good grip, Chip."

"Thanks! Please have a seat."

As instructed, the customer service gal brought in a plate of doughnuts and a pot of fresh coffee.

"To what do we owe the pleasure of your company?"

The chief didn't answer right away. He wanted to toy with Chip a little. Make him sweat. See him squirm.

"That Mrs. Mack out there working window three?"

"Yes, sir, it sure is."

"Pretty gal."

"Uhm-hmm," said the banker. "Pretty as a peach. If, you know, you find seasonal summer fruits attractive."

The chief leaned back in the leather chair. Listened to its rich crinkle. "I didn't know you worked Saturdays, Chip."

"Oh, yes, indeedy. We're open ten to three. Makes it easier for working folks to do their banking, and the ones with jobs are the ones who actually have money. Heh, heh, heh."

When Weitzel laughed, the chief got a whiff of something minty and fresh.

"You weren't here last Saturday," said the police chief.

"Pardon?"

"I came in last weekend. You weren't here."

"Riiiiight," said Weitzel, flipping backward through his desk calendar. "Last Saturday. Right. Almost forgot.

Big bank management symposium. I was out of town. Business trip. Now, what can I do you for, chief?"

"Need a loan."

"All righty. Home improvements?"

"Nope."

"New car?"

"Nope."

"College tuition for your boy?"

"Nope. I need a small business loan."

"And what sort of business are we talking about?"

"A surefire moneymaker."

"Well, we like those. What exactly does this business do?"

"Sorry. That's confidential."

"Well, how much money were you looking for?"

"Ten thousand dollars."

Mr. Weitzel pushed a stack of forms across the desk.

"All righty. I just need you to fill in this loan application."

"No you don't, Chip."

"Uh, yes. Sorry. We do. The bank always needs paperwork to process—"

"Not for this. This is a very unique, very lucrative business opportunity that more or less fell into my lap. You in or out?"

"Well, John, I'm not sure. This is very out of the ordinary. To come and ask the bank to loan you—"

"I don't want the bank's money, Chip. I want yours."

"Excuse me?"

"You got ten thousand dollars to spare, don't you? Shoot, you probably got that much tucked away somewhere in your desk drawer."

Got him. The chief could see Weitzel's Adam's apple bob up and down as he gulped.

"Suppose I was interested in your, uh, proposition?" The banker's voice sounded squeaky. "What would you offer as collateral to guarantee the loan?"

The chief reached into his back pants pocket. Pulled out a folded-over, crumpled envelope.

"These."

He turned the envelope upside down. A dozen grainy security camera photos tumbled out.

"What are they?" said Weitzel, pretending not to know what he was looking at.

"Pictures of you. Last weekend. In Las Vegas. Gambling with a whole mess of cash that may not have been yours. You see, Chip, I may spend *my* weekends in Fairview, but I have friends everywhere."

"POPCORN! PEANUTS! CRACKER JACK!"

That afternoon, Briana played her part with great gusto. It was as if Shakespeare were up in the stands of the high school baseball stadium hawking food.

"Hot, buttery popcorn! Slightly salted peanuts! Crrrr-acker Jackkkkk!" She hit that final consonant so hard, it sounded like someone had just thwacked a home run.

Riley was down on the field in his school photographer disguise: safari vest, backward Furriers baseball cap, big boxy camera to block his face. The camera also had an extremely long lens so he could zoom in on Gavin Brown and see which cheerleader *he* was zooming in on.

"Do you guys see what I'm seeing?" asked Mongo over Riley's Bluetooth earpiece. Mongo was seated two rows behind Brown and blending in nicely with the freshmen. "Every time the frizzy-haired blonde in the middle moves, Gavin moves his head."

"Yeah," said Riley. "Bree?"

"Talk to me," Briana whispered back. Earlier, Jake had linked up their three cell phones through a dial-in conference call service so they could remain in constant contact with one another during the game.

"The frizzy-haired blond cheerleader," said Riley. "The one they tossed up to the top when they made the pyramid."

"Shorty?"

"Yeah. Who is she?"

"Don't know."

"Can you find out?"

"But of course."

"We just need a name," said Riley, pretending to snap a photo of the crowd, actually framing up Gavin Brown. He was wearing a Furriers baseball jersey with the sleeves cut off and had painted half his face brown, the other half white—the team colors. With his flat, round face, he looked like one of those black-and-white cookies—half chocolate, half vanilla.

Briana worked her way down the bleachers to where

the rowdy juniors and seniors were chanting and stomping along with the cheerleaders.

"Here we go, Furriers, here we go!"

Stomp, stomp.

"Here we go, Furriers, here we go!"

Stomp, stomp.

Yes, unlike football, basketball, or even lacrosse, baseball basically had one cheer. On the plus side, most fans already had it memorized.

"Excuse me," Riley heard Briana say to somebody on his earpiece. "I think that girl down there is, like, my second cousin twice removed."

Riley tilted his lens down. Found Briana, who was schmoozing a hunky high schooler while pointing at the frizzy-haired cheerleader, who was shaking her fake-fur pompoms.

"But, and this is, like, totally embarrassing," Briana improvised, "I can't remember her name!" She added a giggle.

"You mean Rebecca? Rebecca Drake?"

"Right. Becca! That's what we call her at family reunions. Becca Boo. The Beckster. Beck-o-matic. Thanks! Here. On the house."

She gave the guy a free box of Cracker Jack.

"Way to go, B," said Riley.

"Now what?"

"Stand by. Mongo?"

"Yeah?"

"Shout, 'Rebecca Drake stinks,' then duck."

"But she doesn't stink, Riley. In fact, I think she is a very talented cheerleader. Very pretty, too. I can see why Gavin keeps staring at her."

"Mongo?"

"Yes, Briana?"

"It's called acting! Act!"

"Oh. Okay."

"Wait for my cue," said Riley as he panned up the crowd to Gavin. Unfortunately, at that moment, their mark was stuffing a whole hot dog slathered with mustard into his mouth.

"You watching Gavin, Bree?" Riley asked.

"Yep."

"Me, too. Okay. Go for it, Mongo."

Mongo cupped his hands around his mouth and shouted, "Rebecca Drake stinks!" He quickly tucked his head down between his knees.

Gavin whipped around. "Who said that?" Now he stood up. "Which one of you jerks said Rebecca stinks?"

"Shout, 'Down in front,'" Riley coached Mongo.

"With my head between my knees?"

"Yes! Briana? Pick up on it!"

"Down in front!" shouted Mongo.

"Down in front! Down in front!" chanted Briana, even though she was in the aisle with a food tray strapped around her neck, not sitting behind Gavin Brown.

"Who said it?" Gavin hollered again.

Now he really was blocking people's view, and the Furriers' best batter, Samuel Justus, was at the plate looking like he was ready to knock one out of the park, so everybody joined in the refrain:

"Down in front, dork face, down in front!"

Stomp, stomp.

"Down in front, dork face, down in front!"

Stomp, stomp.

Flapping his hand at the whole crowd, Gavin finally sat down.

Riley grinned. Maybe it was a good thing baseball had so few cheers. The fans were always hungry for a new one.

The slugger at the plate hit a home run. The crowd rose to its feet. The bleachers rocked with joy. Everybody, including Gavin Brown, immediately forgot how some loudmouth had insulted the perky blond cheerleader.

"Our work here is done," said Riley. "Extricate at your earliest convenience. Rendezvous in fifteen minutes at Jake's place."

"Riley?" asked Mongo sheepishly.

"Yeah?"

"How do I extricate?"

"It means 'get out,'" said Briana.

"Oh, okay. But the game isn't over."

"You're right," said Riley. "It's just getting started."

AROUND SIX P.M., RILEY'S CREW, joined by Jamal Wilson, reassembled in the basement of Jake Lowenstein's house.

Riley remembered when he had first met Jake. In fifth grade, Jake Lowenstein was the shy new kid without any friends who always sat in the back of any classroom. Riley, who, like so many military kids, had once moved six times and attended six different schools in a single school year, never forgot what it felt like to be the new kid with zero friends. So, one day in late September, he sat down at the desk next to Jake's and started peppering the hooded genius with whispered questions while, up at the front of the classroom, the teacher, Mrs. Finkel—who was close to retirement and extremely hard of hearing—tapped a globe with her wooden pointer and droned on about longitude and latitude.

"Hey," Riley whispered to Jake, "what do people in China call their good plates? Hey, is it true cannibals don't eat clowns because they taste funny? Hey, you ever wonder what disease cured ham actually had?"

That's the one that finally made Jake smile. "Hey," he whispered back, "what do you call a male ladybug?"

That one cracked Riley up, and they'd been friends ever since.

Now Jake's house was where Riley, Jamal, and Mongo would be spending the night so they could get up bright and early on Sunday morning to finally start the door-to-door search for Noodle.

Or so they had told their parents.

Briana, on the other hand, didn't have to tell her mom and dad much. They were earthy-crunchies. Aging hippies with severe tree-hugging tendencies. They both wore a lot of beads and clothes made out of hemp and encouraged Briana to "blossom wherever she was planted," which basically meant she didn't have a curfew but always had to carry an extra granola bar in her backpack in case she missed dinner.

"Jamal," said Riley. "Good to see you. Thanks for lending a hand."

"My pleasure, Riley Mack. We're gonna bust that old lady for scratchin' up my iPods, am I right?"

Riley nodded. "We will. Soon as Gavin turns over Noodle."

"Sure. I understand. You need to prioritize. You know what that word means?"

"Yeah. First things first." Riley rubbed his hands together and paced around the basement rumpus room, which Jake had tweaked out with maybe six different custom-made computers, all sorts of monitors, blinking routers, cables everywhere, and, of course, Jedi posters on the wood-paneled walls. Jake was extremely nerdly. In the good way.

"You have Rebecca Drake's number?"

"Check," said Jake.

"Man, we had that in like two seconds," boasted Jamal.

Jake arched an eyebrow. "We?"

"I meant Jake. You shoulda seen him clacking that keyboard, tapping into some kind of database that looked like a swimming pool full of glowing green numbers. My man Jake has wicked mad skills, y'all."

"Yeah," said Briana. "We know."

"Okay," said Riley, still pacing, "what would a high school cheerleader's favorite radio station be?"

"Easy," said Jamal. "Z One Hundred. Got that DJ from *American Idol*. Plays songs by that fifteen-year-old with the curly hair and dimples. Chicks dig the curly hair and dimples, man."

Jake was glued to the computer screen, scanning the results of his most recent internet search. "Jamal's right. According to the ratings data, Z One Hundred is top with teens in the metro area. Says so on their website. Good job, kid."

"That's because I know my demographics," said Jamal. "Find them fascinating. Do you know what—"

"Vital or social statistics of the human population," said Briana before Jamal could finish asking if anybody knew what *demographics* meant.

Riley barged in: "Briana? Can you do a Z One Hundred DJ voice?"

"Shuuuuuure," she said, the single word coming out silky and smooth. "'I'm playing the hits while you're spraying your pits.' That's for a morning DJ."

"Jake? Patch a landline phone into your digital recorder. Briana, the Z One Hundred DJ, is going to call Rebecca Drake."

"This. Is. Zeeeee *One Hundred*," said Briana, getting into character.

"Good," said Riley. "Tell Rebecca she's about to win the one-hundred dollar jackpot. That'll get her talking, even if she's still supposed to be cheering. Maybe ask her a couple trivia questions. Music junk. Get her gabbing."

Briana nodded.

"You'll need enough material so you can imitate her voice."

"So I can call Gavin!"

"Exactly." Riley powered up the digital camera. "We need Brown's cell number, too," he said to Jake.

"Already got it."

"I told you he had mad skills," said Jamal.

Riley flipped his camera around so Briana could check out the display screen. He thumbed through a couple of the close-ups he took of Gavin at the game. Briana cringed when Riley flashed her the hot-dog-stuffing shot.

"Faunky."

"Yeah. Jamal? You get on that other computer. Find the high school sports site, track the game. Thirty minutes after it's over, when Briana has Rebecca's voice down cold, she calls Gavin."

Briana had her eyes closed and was mumbling, "In my circles, in my circles"—something she always mumbled right before she "went on."

"Now, Briana," Riley continued, "when you get Gavin on the line, tell him how amazing he looked in his ripped-sleeve jersey and Furriers face paint. How you'd like to go out on a date with him."

Briana pried open an eye. "Fine. Just make sure somebody has a barf bucket standing by."

"Lay it on thick. Tell Gavin he'll make you the happiest girl in the whole wide world if he just does one iddy-biddy thing. . . ."

"Gives you a goldendoodle puppy!" shouted Mongo.

Riley smiled slyly. "Mongo, I like the way you think."

"Because you already thought it, right?"

Riley shrugged. "Whatever. Jake—initiate the call to Rebecca Drake."

"On it." Jake slipped on his headphones and pressed the red button on the digital recorder.

"The digits are rolling," added Jamal.

"You ready, Briana?"

"This is such a fabbomatic plan, Riley!" she gushed. "Your best ever!"

"Ringing," said Jake.

"Tell her she could be a winner," whispered Riley.

"Yeah," said Mongo. "So we can turn Gavin Brown into a big fat loser!"

20

AT SEVEN O'CLOCK ON SATURDAY night, half an hour after the baseball game ended, Gavin Brown was sitting in his bedroom picking at the flaky white gunk between his toes.

It was his favorite part of the day—scratching his feet, sniffing his fingernails.

His mom was downstairs, snoring on the couch. She'd already scratched her feet for the night.

His dad was out somewhere on police business.

Gavin yawned. It had been a long, long day. Some of his favorite cartoons had double episodes in the morning and then he had to go to the playground in Sherman Green to work on his weekly quota. He jumped some first graders, stole their tricycles and bouncy balls. Scored a couple tennis balls from old farts flinging them for dogs to chase after. Tomorrow, he'd hit more playgrounds. Try to snatch purses from moms busy changing diapers.

His cell phone rang. Gavin snapped open the phone.

"Hello?"

"Hi, is this Gavin?"

"Yes. Who is this?"

"Rebecca."

"Who?"

"Rebecca Drake, silly. You know—goooo, team!"

Ohmygod. Gavin could not believe this. Rebecca Drake, the girl of his dreams, was calling him. On a Saturday night. On the telephone. Why wasn't she out on a date with Samuel Justus, the slugger who smacked three home runs in the game? Why was the golden goddess calling him instead? Gavin was so nervous, air was whistling through his nose hairs.

"That's a pretty song," cooed Rebecca.

"Huh?"

"That song you're whistling."

"Oh, thanks."

"I saw you this afternoon, Gavin."

"Huh? Where?"

"At the game, silly."

Oh, yeah. It was definitely Rebecca. She called a lot

of boys "silly," especially the ones she liked. Gavin had wandered the halls behind her for a couple weeks now. She wore nice perfume. Smelled like walking bubble gum.

"I loved how you painted your face brown and white!" Rebecca gushed. "That shows true school spirit and I'm, like, a cheerleader, so that much school spirit means an awful lot to me."

"Did you like my shirt?"

"The shirt was amazingly awesome, Gavbo. Can I call you Gavbo, Gavin?"

He gulped before he answered. "Sure."

"I especially liked the stringy threads under your armpits where you cut off the sleeves."

"Thanks. I didn't use scissors. I just tore 'em off."

"Awesome! Anyway, me and my girlfriends . . ."

"Those other cheerleaders?"

"Yeah. Anyway, we were, you know, chilling after the game and, like, talking and junk and, like, Sherry—she's, like, the one on my left . . ."

"Oh, yeah. She's cute."

Ooops. Mistake.

"But not as cute as you, Rebecca. You're the cutest."

"Yeah. I know. Anyway, Sherry said she, like, heard that you're the kind of guy who can get a girl anything she wants."

"Where'd she hear that?"

"Around."

"Well, she's two hundred percent correct! You name it, I can get it for you!"

"Really? Because I'd really like to hang out with you, Gavbo. So, if you do this one iddy-biddy thing for me . . ."

Gavin stood up straight. "What is it you want, Rebecca?"

"A goldendoodle!"

"What's that?"

"A dog, silly. You know—part golden retriever, part poodle."

"A golden poodle?"

"Doodle!"

"I never heard of such a thing. It's a dog?"

Rebecca giggled. "Are you playing games with me, Gavin?"

"No, I swear. I don't know about any goldendoodles but I could go buy you one. Where do they sell them?"

"Come on, Gavbo. Sherry said you were the man. That you probably already had a goldendoodle. A puppy? Wears a pink sparkly collar?"

"I have a couple golden watches. They sparkle."

"I want a goldendoodle! A cutiful doggy just like the one on all those Lost Dog posters all over town?"

"Sorry. I haven't seen those."

"What, are you, like, totally blind or something?"

"Don't be mad at me, Rebecca, please? I'll find you a goldendoodle, okay? I promise!"

"Where?"

"I'm not sure! But if you want a goldendoodle, I'll get you a goldendoodle—even if I have to steal it!"

And Rebecca hung up on him.

"WELL, THAT WAS JUST CRAPTACULAR," said Briana.

"You did a very good job," said Jake, who had listened to both sides of the conversation on his headphones. "You matched Rebecca's voice perfectly."

"But Gavin swears he doesn't even know what a goldendoodle is; doesn't know one was just stolen."

"Maybe he's telling the truth, y'all," added Jamal.

"Yeah," Riley mumbled. "Guess there's a first time for everything."

"He really didn't steal my mom's dog?" asked Mongo sadly.

"I don't think so," said Jake.

"Me neither," added Briana.

"Then who did?"

"That, my friend," said Riley, "is the question."

Riley sank down into a beanbag chair. Tried to keep cool. But this was bad. Real bad. His big scheme had just gone bust. He'd wasted everybody's Saturday and come up empty.

But getting mad at himself for blowing the rescue mission wouldn't help. What was it his dad always said? "Regret is a waste of energy. You can't build on regret; it's only for wallowing in." Riley was certain someone like Churchill or Shakespeare said it before his dad but, still, it made sense. Wallowing was something a pig did. Rolling around in the mud because it feels good and because a pig is, basically, a walking slab of bacon.

So Riley knew not to waste time feeling sorry for himself. He needed to figure out what to do next. He rubbed his cheeks. Tortured his hair. He thought. Then, he thought harder.

He had built Operation Blind Date on a faulty assumption.

But if Gavin Brown hadn't stolen the dog, who had?

Did Noodle just run away when Emma opened the gate?

If so, how come Grandma Brown had the dog's sparkling pink collar for sale in her antiques tent?

He glanced around the rumpus room. His crew

looked brokenhearted. Defeated. Jake, Briana, Mongo, even chatty Jamal, were sitting there, silently staring at their shoes.

They needed Riley.

And he needed a new plan.

A new clue.

"Somebody had to steal Noodle," mumbled Mongo.

"Yeah," said Briana. "A space alien on a rocket ship, remember?"

Riley's eyes brightened.

"Jake?" he said.

"Yeah?"

"What time is it?"

"Seven twenty. Why?"

"Call the Pizza Palace. See if they're still open."

"We're having a crisis and you're ordering pizza?" said Briana. "Honestly, Riley. At least act like you care what happens to Noodle."

"Make the call, Jake. Please."

"What's up, Riley Mack?" asked Jamal, the first to spring out of his chair. "You just hatched a new plan, didn't you?"

Riley held up a hand, focused on Jake. "Hang on."

"Uh, yeah—how late are you guys open tonight?" Jake asked whoever answered the phone at the pizza place. "Nine?"

"Ask them if Nick is working tonight."

"Hey, is my buddy Nick working there tonight?"

Riley flashed Jake a thumbs-up. Adding that "buddy" bit was a smooth move.

"Okay. Cool. Uh, yeah, I think we're going to order a pie but I have to find out who wants what. Call you right back, dude." He thumbed the off button. "What's up, Riley?"

"Nick. The Pizza Palace busboy. We saw him, remember? Outside the pet shop."

"Oh, yeah," said Mongo. "He had those two bird-cages. Pink and blue."

Riley nodded. "And he said something like, 'Hey, Mongo, sorry about your mom's dog, man.'"

"Yeah," said Mongo. "I thought that was very considerate of him."

Riley refound his foxy swagger. "So, Mongo—how'd Nick know your mom lost her dog?"

"I dunno. I guess he read the poster."

Riley ambled over to where Jake had a stack of Lost Dog flyers piled beside a computer printer.

"Oh, you mean this poster? The one where we specifically left off your mother's name and only printed her phone number? You think maybe Nick has your home telephone number memorized? You think, maybe, he sees this number, the only identifying information on the whole poster, by the way, and, boom, he instantly knows it's your mom's dog that's gone missing?"

125

"Whahoobi!" said Briana. "Brilliant!"

"And don't forget, guys," Riley continued, "Nick was there last Friday at the Pizza Palace, when Mongo first told Jake and me how much his mom spent on Noodle. Nick was eavesdropping. Fishing for a sitting duck."

"Dude," said Jamal, "now you're the one mixing metaphors."

"Sorry. I do that sometimes when I get excited."

"But, Riley," said Jake, "how did the dog's collar end up at the flea market this morning? Is Nick somehow connected to Grandma Brown?"

"He has to be," said Riley, pacing around the room. "He said something else that maybe he shouldn't have when we bumped into him on Main Street. He told us he had another job, doing 'this and that.'"

"So maybe 'this,'" said Briana, "is stealing dogs."

"And 'that,'" added Mongo, "is giving them to Gavin's grandmother!"

"Jamal? Briana?" said Riley. "Grab your backpacks. You two are coming with me. Mongo, Jake—hang tight."

"Where you guys going?" asked Mongo.

"Where else? The Pizza Palace."

AT 7:30 ON SATURDAY NIGHT, Otto and Fred, the suburban bank robbers, were hungry.

The only food at the cheap motel where they were staying was hanging off pegs in a vending machine. Fig Newtons, Pop-Tarts, or microwavable popcorn. And there was no microwave in their room.

"You wanna go grab a pizza or something?" suggested Fred.

"Yeah. Let's head downtown. That place we saw near the bank."

They drove their battered blue van the few blocks from the low-rent motel to Main Street.

Fairview being a sleepy suburban town, even on a

Saturday night, they had two dozen parking meters to pick from. Otto was chewing a fresh toothpick. Fred was cracking his "neck knuckles." The two men climbed out of the van and breathed in the fresh, suburban air.

"Looks like they roll up the sidewalks pretty early in this burb," said Otto, surveying the empty streets.

"Means we can get an early start Thursday night."

Otto nodded. "Come on. I'm starving."

They approached the glowing windows of the Pizza Palace. A sign dangling in the window said, YES, WE'RE OPEN.

Otto shoved open the door. Fred followed after him.

"Can we help you gentlemen?"

It was a police officer. He was sitting at a table in the center of the dining room, his butt cheeks sagging over the sides of his seat like saddlebags.

There was an old woman sitting to his left, her grouchy face circled by a red-checkered head scarf.

To Tubbo Cop's right was a pimply-faced geek with greasy black hair tucked up under a hairnet. The kid was wearing a tomato-sauce-splattered apron over his shabby white T-shirt.

"I said, can we help you gentlemen?" the cop repeated.

"Yeah," said Otto. "Pepperoni, onions, and peppers. To go."

"We're closed," said Pimples, who appeared to be

seventeen, maybe eighteen.

"That so?" said Fred. "How come the sign in the window says Open?"

"Sign's wrong," said the cop, standing up—bringing the chair with him the first six inches because it was sweat-glued to his butt. He pointed to the sauce-speckled schlub. "Nick closed early."

Now the cop started squinting hard at Fred and Otto, like maybe he recognized their faces.

Like maybe he had seen some wanted posters circulated by cops back in the Buckeye State.

"Sorry to bother you, folks," said Otto.

"We're not really hungry," added Fred.

Then the two of them dashed out the door.

Chief Brown smiled as the two strangers hurried out of the pizza shop.

He still had *It*. The ability to boss ordinary bums around, to tell the weaklings of this world what they could do and when they could do it. If he were the one over in Afghanistan, instead of "heroic Colonel Mack," that war would've been won in a week. But not everybody could go gallivanting around the world playing soldier. Somebody had to stay home and keep the economy humming.

"Lock the door," he snapped at Nick.

"Yes, sir."

"And take down that stupid sign!"

"All right," said the sheriff's mother, reconvening their little meeting after the brief interruption, "we have ten thousand dollars from the banker." She spit tobacco juice into a paper cup. "We're just about ready to get into the goldendoodle business!"

"Great," said the chief, "because I checked out what Nick heard that idiot Mongo Montgomery say to his pals: every puppy Noodle cranks out will fetch us at least fifteen hundred bucks, most of it pure profit!"

"Don't get cocky, son. We still need to be careful. Play this thing smart. We ship puppies to out-of-state customers only. No local sales. We don't want a bunch of looky-loos nosing around my operation out at the farm." She screwed down her tiny eyes. "Now then, we need to take the next step: we need to find Noodle a mate."

"Hey," said Nick, "maybe I should just go steal another goldendoodle, a boy this time."

"No," said Grandma Brown. "We want to breed what they call a backcross goldendoodle."

"A what?" asked the chief.

"Offspring of a goldendoodle and a *poodle*. A back-cross hybrid is even less likely to shed. Better for rich people whose kids have allergies. We can charge sixteen, maybe seventeen hundred per puppy. Then we screw 'em for another four hundred bucks on the shipping, which costs us maybe fifty."

"So, I need to steal a poodle?" said Nick.

"No." Grandma Brown pulled out a crinkled clipping. "I want this one. Apricot."

She showed the chief an ad for a very kingly-looking standard poodle, one of the big ones.

"How much?"

"He's a champion sire."

"How much, Momma?"

"Whatever it takes! Relax, Johnny. We'll earn it all back. Apricot here will turn Noodle into the goose that lays us our solid gold eggs."

23

AT A QUARTER TO EIGHT, Riley, Briana, and Jamal rode their bikes down Main Street.

The darkened town was deserted.

"You guys?" said Riley. "Let's take the alley!"

He swung his bike hard to the right. Briana and Jamal followed.

"You think Nick's still in the Pizza Palace?" whispered Briana as they pedaled through the puddles pockmarking the gravel alleyway behind the brick walls and back doors of Main Street's shops.

"There's his delivery moped," said Riley, pointing out a scooter with a pop-top cargo carrier mounted over the rear bumper. The moped was leaning up against the Pizza Palace's big green Dumpster.

"Park here," said Riley, bringing his bike to a skidding stop behind Fairview Fluff and Fold, the Laundromat next door to the Pizza Palace. Riley swung off his bicycle seat, slung his backpack off his shoulders, and toed open his kickstand. Briana and Jamal did the same.

"Now what?" asked Briana when the bikes were all tucked into the shadows.

"I'm not exactly sure," said Riley.

"What?"

Riley gave her a playful wink. "You know me, Bree. I kind of make this stuff up as I go along."

"You have what they call an impulsive or improvisational spirit," said Jamal. "Am I right?"

"Yeah."

"That's cool. I'm all about staying loosey-goosey."

"Jamal?" said Briana.

"Yeah?"

"Do you ever not talk?"

"Not really. I suffer from what they call logorrhea, an excessive flow of words. Some call it diarrhea of the mouth."

"Gross."

"I don't like it either, but—"

"You guys?" Riley put a finger to his lips.

Crouching low, he slunk quietly up the alleyway. Briana and Jamal slunk after him. They made it to the rear entrance of the Pizza Palace and pressed their backs up against the swirled stucco walls.

"Briana?"

"Yeah?"

"Go around front. Keep Nick busy. Order a pizza or something."

"Excellent! And right before he slides the pie into the oven, I'll change my mind. 'Oh, I'm sorry, I forgot. I'm a vegetarian! Can you take off the sausage I just ordered?' And when he does that, I'll say, 'Wait. My brother *loves* sausage. Make it half veggie, half sausage!'"

"Works for me," said Riley. "Go!"

Briana slipped sideways up the tight breezeway between the pizza place and the Laundromat.

"So, you figured out what we do next?" whispered Jamal. "If not, I got a couple ideas. One. We go inside and grab a couple slices. I'm starving. Two—"

"Jamal?" Riley's head bobbed toward the motor scooter. "Can you pop open that cargo box?"

"Is a pig pork?" said Jamal as he pulled a soft cloth wallet out of his back pocket. It held all sorts of slender metal tools that sort of looked like a combination of nail files and dental instruments. "C'mon. Let's go crack that sucker open."

"What do you mean you're closed?" they heard

Briana declare much too loudly from up at the front entrance to the Pizza Palace. "Your advertisements clearly state that you are open until nine!" She was loudly enunciating every word so Riley and Jamal would know what was going on inside the building.

"Hurry," said Riley as Jamal worked a metal pick with a squiggly head into the keyhole.

"You know," said Jamal, jiggling the stainless steel tool, "this cargo carrier is big enough to hold a puppy."

"I know," said Riley. "Come on. Open it."

"Hi, Nick!" they heard Briana shout from out on the sidewalk. "How are your parakeets? Is that a new T-shirt? Oh, I like the hairnet, too."

The lid on the hard plastic trunk sprang open.

"What's that?" said Jamal.

Riley reached in and pulled out a rubber Halloween mask.

"Meet Emma's Martian," he said, holding up a green alien face with two Ping-Pong-ball-sized eyes; a tall, wrinkled forehead; and stubs where his antennae had broken off.

Riley zipped open his backpack and found his miniature flashlight. He shone its beam around the inside of the hard-shelled carrier. The light glinted off a clump of shiny, curled hairs.

"Noodle's golden locks," said Riley.

"You want to tag and bag the forensic evidence?" asked Jamal.

"No need. We know Nick did it. And this motor scooter? That's what made those puttering rocketship sounds Emma told me about."

"Miss Bloomfield," a voice boomed from the front of the Pizza Palace. "Where are your hippy-dippy parents?"

Riley, of course, recognized the voice. The blowhard. Police Chief Brown.

"At home, sir. Watching that movie about Woodstock. Again."

"Go watch it with them. This restaurant is closed."

"Yes, Chief Brown," Briana chanted in a singsong voice meant to be heard a block away. "Sorry, Chief Brown. I was just hungry for pizza, Chief Brown. Say, who is that attractive elderly woman spitting into the paper cup?"

"*My* mother. Now go home before I call yours!"

Good work, Riley thought. Briana had let him know Grandma Brown was in the house, further cementing the connection between Grandma, Nick, and the stolen dog.

Riley's eyes swept up and down the dark lane.

There was a boxy truck parked at the far end of the alleyway. As his eyes adjusted, Riley could read

Grandma's Antiques painted in frilly letters over the cab.

He whipped out his cell phone. Speed-dialed Jake. Phone pressed to his ear with one hand, he grabbed his backpack with the other and sprinted toward the truck. Jamal was sprinting right beside him.

Jake picked up. "Riley?"

"Hey. If I turn on the GPS locator in a cell phone, can you track it?"

"Definitely. If I know the number and we spend a few bucks on one of the web-based tracking services, we can follow it wherever it goes."

"Cool. Hang on. Jamal?"

"Yeah?"

"Come with me."

They scooted around to the rear of the truck. The roll-down door was shut and secured with a combination lock.

"You want me to pop this lock, too?"

"Exactly."

"So, tell me, Riley Mack: Is this some kind of initiation or something? If I pass, can I join your crew?"

"Just crack the lock, okay?"

"I got you. We're gonna steal back all the fifth-grade loot Grandma's been peddling in her tent, right?"

"No. I want to add something to her stash."

"Add something?"

"Yeah."

"You're whacked, you know that, Riley Mack?"

"Yeah. Come on. Hurry."

Jamal grabbed hold of the combination lock and pulled down hard to tighten the hasp. Riley thumbed the controls on his cell. Turned off all the alerts. Activated the GPS.

"Can you do that any faster, Jamal?"

"Maybe. If I, you know, didn't have to answer so many questions while I was doing it." Jamal clicked the dial clockwise. Felt it stick. Moved two numbers farther. Rotated the dial counterclockwise. Found the second sticking point. Now he clacked it clockwise until it hit the sweet spot.

The lock popped open.

"Ten seconds. New personal best. That fast enough for you, Riley Mack?"

"Yeah. Thanks. Help me shove this thing open."

They maneuvered the rolling door up an inch or two.

"Wait," said Riley. "Close it."

"What? I thought we were opening it."

"Close it and lock it!"

"I just unlocked it."

"I know."

"Oh, you're being all loosey-goosey again, aren't you?"

"No. I just realized that if I toss my cell phone into the back of Grandma's truck, she'll find it."

"And sell it," added Jamal.

Riley nodded. "Hang on, Jake."

"I'm hanging."

"Jamal, see if there's a good spot under the truck to stash a cell phone."

The wiry little fifth grader slithered under the bumper. "We could put it on top of the muffler. Of course, it might bounce off. Be better if we had some duct tape or something to strap it down with."

Riley pulled a roll of silver duct tape out of his backpack. Tapped Jamal on the knee with it. "Here you go."

Jamal's hand found the tape. "You carry duct tape with you all the time, Riley Mack?"

"Yeah. There's nothing it can't do." He put his phone to his ear. "Get ready, Jake."

"Wait a second. What number do you want me to tail?"

"Mine."

Riley handed his cell phone to Jamal, who quickly taped it on top of the muffler, then crawled out from underneath the truck.

"Let's go," said Riley. They ran back to the moped and Dumpster, where Briana was anxiously waiting for them.

"Where were you guys?"

Riley smiled. "Up the alley."

"Doing what?"

"Helping Grandma Brown lead us to wherever she hid Noodle."

LATE SATURDAY, JAKE'S GPS TRACKING software showed the truck leaving Fairview and traveling about ten miles out into the country, where it remained parked all night.

"You think that's where she has Noodle?" asked Mongo.

"Tomorrow night, we'll know for sure," said Riley.

"How we gonna do that, Riley Mack?" asked Jamal, his eyes fixed on the static star in the center of the glowing map.

"Easy. We're going out there."

And then Riley explained to Briana what she had to do to help make that happen.

* * *

On Sunday afternoon, Riley and his mom went to the flea market in Sherman Green.

"This is nice, Riley. I've been cooped up in that stuffy bank all week. It feels good to be out in the fresh air."

"I figured you might need a break."

"You figured right."

"Riley? Mrs. Mack?"

It was Briana and her mother. Right on schedule. Two fifteen p.m. in front of the goat-yogurt stand.

"Well, hello, Briana," said Riley's mom. "Moonbeam."

Yes, Briana's mother's name was Moonbeam. It probably wasn't on her birth certificate, but that's what she called herself. Moonbeam Sunchild Bloomfield. She was wearing a tie-dyed dress that went down to her ankles, lots of beads, rose-tinted sun goggles, and a flower-power headband that put a crimp in her bubbly gray Afro.

"Hey," she said slowly. "What's happenin'?"

"Not much," said Riley's mom. "Just, you know, checking out the market."

Mrs. Bloomfield nodded very slowly, very thoughtfully. "Far out."

"You betcha," said Riley's mom.

"Oh, Riley," said Briana, "I almost forgot. . . ."

Riley tried not to grin. "Yes?"

"I have to do that astronomy project tonight."

142

"Oh, the one Mr. Thorne gave us where you have to go out into the country and check out the constellations and junk?"

"Yes," said Briana, playing the script to perfection. "Have you done your astronomy project yet?"

"No. Hey, maybe we can do ours together!"

"Cool. Are you free tonight?"

"What time?"

"How about my mom and I pick you up at nine? It'll be way dark then."

Riley turned to his mom. "Is that okay, Mom?"

"What time will you be home?"

"No later than eleven," said Briana.

"You don't mind driving the kids, Moonbeam?" asked Riley's mom.

"Not at all."

"Oh, Mom," said Riley, "I need to borrow Dad's night vision goggles. To see the stars better."

"Okay. Do you know where they are?"

"Yeah. In my room."

At 9:15 p.m., Riley, Briana, Jamal, and Mrs. Bloomfield were parked on a country road in the middle of nowhere, but only a few miles outside the town limits of Fairview.

Jamal, who was only ten, had told his parents that he and his new friend, Jake Lowenstein, were building a supercomputer in Jake's basement.

"Beautiful out here, isn't it?" said Briana's mom.

"Yes, ma'am," said Jamal.

"Listen to the crickets. Soak in their wisdom."

"Well, we gotta go, Mom," said Briana. "The stars are all aligned and junk."

"Should I come with you kids?"

"Um, no. Mr. Thorne, that's our teacher, he's a real stickler about us doing our own homework without a bunch of help from our parental units."

"Groovy." Mrs. Bloomfield put a New Age tinkly-music disc into the dashboard CD player and closed her eyes. "I'll just chill. Haven't done my om chant today."

Riley, Jamal, and Briana headed up a rutted dirt road. They could hear Mrs. Bloomfield *om*ing in the distance.

All through elementary school, Briana Bloomfield had always been one of the most popular girls in whatever school she attended. But then, the minute seventh grade started, for some reason all her girlfriends turned against her, called her Flaky Wakey and Wavy Gravy, like the old Ben & Jerry's ice-cream flavor. Seemed all the other popular girls had decided over the summer that they were way too mature to hang out with Briana Bloomfield any longer.

Riley could tell she needed a brand-new set of friends. So he became the first.

"Sorry about that," Briana now said. "My mom acts a little goofy sometimes. She's actually supersmart. Has a PhD."

"I think she's far out," said Riley with a grin.

"I can dig her, man," added Jamal.

Briana smiled. "Yeah. Me, too."

The road soon narrowed as it entered a stand of tall evergreen trees. Riley, Briana, and Jamal were engulfed by darkness and an eerie quiet. The only sounds were the crunch of their feet and the chirp of bugs serenading Mrs. Bloomfield in her hybrid station wagon.

"You guys?" It was Jake, back in the basement. He had lent Riley one of his spare cell phones and hooked everybody up with linked earpieces.

"Yeah?" said Riley.

"You're close. I'd say it's only about another hundred yards to where she parked the truck. And Riley? You better move fast. The battery in your cell phone must be tanking. The GPS signal is spotty. Intermittent."

"Got you."

"You guys find Noodle?" asked Mongo, stationed in the basement with Jake.

"Not yet, big guy," said Riley. "But don't worry— we're not coming back without her."

"Thanks," said Mongo, sounding kind of choked up.

"Hey, you'd do the same for us," said Jamal. "Am I right? Say I needed to employ a little muscle to get

145

back a couple iPods or something . . ."

"Jamal?" said Riley. "Focus."

Off in the distance, Riley thought he heard a dog bark.

Briana's eyebrows shot up. She heard it, too.

"Come on," said Riley. "It's showtime."

A gated fence blocked the way forward. The air was scented with the odor of wet hay and wetter animals. On the other side was probably some kind of farm. Riley shone his compact flashlight at a padlock clamped through a loop of heavy chain.

"I got it," said Jamal.

"Hurry," said Riley.

Jamal worked a jagged steel pick into the lock. "Ooh. This is a good one. Gonna take a little longer than that cheap motor scooter pop-top."

"You guys?" It was Briana. Over in the bushes. Holding open a hole in the chain-link fence.

"Good eye," said Riley. "Come on, Jamal. Let's go."

"Wait a second," said Jamal, twisting and flicking the tool jammed inside the padlock. "Almost got it."

"We don't need to do that anymore. There's a hole in the fence."

"Fine. Sure. Some people are always looking for the easy way."

They scrambled through the brambles.

Briana was already on the other side of the fence.

Jamal crawled through the hole next, muttering about shortcuts and laziness. Riley was the last one through and made sure to rig the fencing so the breach didn't show. He tore a small sliver of silver duct tape off its roll, wrapped it around a link in the fence.

"So we can spot it later," he said. "We might be in a hurry."

Because Granny Brown might be chasing after them. With a shotgun or, seeing how she was a farmer, a pitchfork.

Up ahead, through an opening in the trees, Riley could see a weedy meadow and, beyond that, the silhouette of a short outbuilding of some sort. It was wide, but not very tall. Maybe a chicken coop. Maybe a huge rabbit hutch. The air was fetid. It reeked like the cattle tent at the county fair. Or the urinal in the boys' bathroom at school.

"Somebody's coming!" whispered Briana.

"Two somebodies," added Jamal. "I hear voices."

"Going to night vision," said Riley, flipping down the lenses on his dad's very expensive goggles, which allowed him to see in the dark. He panned to the left, where he saw two green-gray images. Fat man. Waddling woman. He heard their muffled voices. Followed them as they neared the chicken coop.

That's when Riley saw the dogs.

Dozens and dozens of dogs.

"SHUT UP, YOU MANGY MUTTS!" shouted Chief Brown as he whacked the wooden frame of a raised chicken coop.

Only it wasn't a chicken coop.

It was a dog coop.

Through the night vision goggles, Riley could make out two rows of elevated cages, each cage maybe three feet wide and three feet deep with very little headroom. There were ten cages in each row, with three or four dogs squeezed into each and every cage.

Sixty, seventy dogs.

Mostly puppies. Some older. Some crippled.

Now that Chief Brown had rattled their cages, the

barks and cries of distress were deafening.

"Shut your yapping traps or nobody gets dinner!" shouted Grandma Brown. She went to a nearby post and flicked up a circuit breaker. Sparks sputtered. Spotlights blazed to life to illuminate all the miserable creatures locked in their even more miserable cages. The infrared signature of the lighting was so intense, Riley had to flip up the night vision goggles to keep from frying his retinas.

"Dag," whispered Jamal.

The horror of the dogs trapped in their filthy cages might have been the first thing to ever leave Jamal Wilson speechless.

"Riley," whispered Briana. "It's a puppy mill!"

The three of them were lying on their stomachs behind the rotted trunk of a fallen tree, maybe twenty yards away from the closest cages.

"We need to get Noodle out of this horrible place!" said Briana.

Riley agreed. But first they had to find her.

"Toss me your field glasses."

Briana lobbed Riley her binoculars. He scanned the rickety chicken-wire cages, which were propped up on wooden stilts so the dogs' poop would fall through the mesh floor to the mud below.

We should rescue them all, Riley thought. But would that be considered stealing, since Grandma Brown technically "owned" the dogs she was abusing?

Okay. Tonight's mission would be a limited one: find and extract Noodle. But Riley knew he'd be coming back for the others—soon.

He could see that some of the dogs, especially the older ones, looked sick. Weeping red sores splotched their fur. Shrunken bellies tugged down on their chest skin, pulling it tight against exposed ribs.

Grandma Brown walked up the center lane between the cages, scooping handfuls of kibble from a five-gallon bucket, tossing it into the cages. Dogs fought one another for the measly scraps of food. Jaws snapped. Hackles shot up. The chorus of desperate dog barks was quickly replaced by the violent snarls of starving beasts.

Riley inched the binoculars to the left and saw Chief Brown, pulling a cell phone out of his bulging shirt pocket.

"Hello?" he shouted to be heard over the dogs. "Yeah. Yeah. I thought we agreed to eight thousand? Aw, never mind. Ship it tonight. Tonight!"

Riley inched the binoculars over to the circuit breaker box. It had no door panel on its front and was mounted on a post maybe two feet in front of a corrugated aluminum shed. Riley tilted the glasses down and noticed a coiled garden hose lying on the ground. It gave him an idea.

"You got your poodle, Mom," said the chief. "Apricot will be here first thing tomorrow morning. Of course those crooks jacked up the price. Cost me *nine* thousand dollars!"

"Aw, quit your bellyaching. We got the goldendoodle for free."

"Yeah, yeah, yeah," groused the chief. "So where is she?"

Grandma Brown head-gestured left. "Gave Noodle a cage of her own. She gets the pink one. Apricot will move into the blue one next door."

There, on the ground, sitting underneath the closest puppy hutch, were two parakeet cages—the same ones they'd seen Nick carrying outside the pet supply store. The baby-blue birdcage was empty but, behind the pink bars, Riley could see a lump of muddy fur curled up in a terrified ball.

Noodle.

"Apricot weighs seventy pounds!" screamed the police chief. "He's not going to fit in a birdcage!"

"So, we'll buy him a big crate!" his mother snapped back.

Noodle's parakeet prison had a chain looped through its thin wire bars. The chain was then wrapped around a four-by-four post and secured with a serious-looking lock.

Riley lowered the binoculars and rolled onto his

back. He touched his earpiece. "Jake?" he said in a hushed voice.

"Yeah?"

"Chief Brown's cell number. We need it."

"On it."

"Briana?"

She scooted closer.

"I need to borrow your video camera."

Briana was the star reporter on FMS-TV, the middle school's TV station, which was basically a bunch of kids who read the announcements every morning in a makeshift news studio set up in a corner of the library. She always carried a tiny Flip Video camera wherever she went.

She dug it out of her backpack. "Here."

Riley took it. "Thanks. Now you've got to pull Chief Brown out of the scene."

"How?"

"You got that cell number, Jake?"

"Yeah."

"Briana—head back to the gate. Get the number from Jake. Call the chief. Tell him he won something. Make it food. The guy likes to eat."

"Cheese of the Month Club!" said Briana in an excited whisper.

"Works for me," Riley whispered back. "But your phone call keeps breaking up. Tell him he's in a bad cell zone. Keep him moving. Toward the farmhouse, away from the cages."

"Gotcha."

"Go! Hurry!"

Ducking low, Briana scampered back the way they had come in. Riley turned to the wiry fifth grader.

"Jamal, you're with me."

"Cool."

"Noodle is in a pink parakeet cage underneath the closest coop. The cage is chained to a four-by-four post—"

"And there's a lock involved, am I right?"

Riley nodded. "I can't tell if it's a combination lock or a key."

"Either way, I'm popping it! But you know, Riley, locks aren't all I do. Say you needed to rig up a . . ."

They heard a hose *snick snick-snick* to life. Jets of water needled against the aluminum sides of the shed.

The chief's cell phone rang.

"Hello? I won what? You're breaking up. Hold on. Can you hear me now? What if I move over here?"

The chief's voice faded in the distance.

"Stay low, stay quiet," Riley said to Jamal. "Stay in the shadows till the lights go out."

"How's that gonna happen?"

"I'm pretty sure Grandma's going to have an electrical accident in about two minutes."

"Cool. I'm down with that."

"When the lights go dark, unlock Noodle's cage, grab it, and haul your butt out of here. Meet up with Briana and head for the car."

"Where you gonna be, Riley Mack?"

"Busy."

"Doing what, man?"

"Well, first, I need to shoot some video. Then, I need to take out those lights."

ABOUT 150 MILES TO THE south, Chip Weitzel found a quiet corner and placed his telephone call.

"Hello?"

"Maddie?" *Cough, cough.* "Chip Weitzel." *Cough, cough.*

"You don't sound so good," said Mrs. Mack.

"Yeah. I know." *Cough. Cough.* "Sorry to be calling you this late on a Sunday night, but I'm gonna need to take a sick day tomorrow."

"I'm sorry you're not feeling well."

"Thanks. I think it's just a bug. One of those twenty-four-hour deals. Should be fine by Tuesday."

Or sooner, he thought, *if my luck changes!*

"Is there anything I can do to help? Do you need any medicines picked up at the drugstore? Chicken soup?"

"No. I've got everything I need here. Thanks. But tomorrow morning, I need you to fill in for me at the bank."

"Oh-kay," Mrs. Mack said hesitantly.

"Don't worry. It's not much extra work. Just need you to open up at eight. Turn on the lights."

"Well, I think I can do that." She sounded relieved.

"Of course, you'll need to go in the back door."

"Oh. Okay."

"And you'll need the security code. Do you have a pen and a piece of paper?"

"Hang on."

He gave her a second. Glanced over to the flashing lights of the casino floor.

"All right," said Mrs. Mack. "I'm all set."

"Good. Write this down, memorize the code, and then eat the paper."

Silence on the other end of the line.

"That was a joke, Maddie."

"Oh."

"You really don't have to eat it. Just destroy it."

"Yes, sir."

"Okay, here we go: two-two-two, three-three-three, four-four-four. Got it?"

"Two-two-two, three-three-three, four-four-four."

Sure, it was a simple code, but Chuck Weitzel was a busy man; he didn't have time to memorize a complex string of numbers.

"And Maddie? I'd appreciate it if I wasn't disturbed tomorrow. Need to get my rest."

"We won't bother you. I promise."

"Thanks. My apologies again for calling so late. I know it's a school night. Riley's probably already asleep, huh?"

"Actually, he's off on a field trip with some friends. They're working on an astronomy project."

"Good for him. Well, I better crawl into bed."

"Feel better."

"Thanks." *Cough. Cough.* "I'll try."

Weitzel powered off his phone.

It would take a miracle for him to feel better.

For the first time since he launched his Casino Based Investment Strategy, he was down. Losing. Having one of those cold streaks all the gamblers who weren't savvy bankers constantly whined about.

And it was all on account of that greedy police chief!

After he had given John Brown the ten-thousand-dollar "small business loan" out of his personal funds, the money stored in his secret safe had shrunk from fifty to forty thousand dollars—a very unhealthy 20 percent dip.

So, Sunday morning, he had grabbed the remaining

money, stuffed it all into a briefcase, and brought it three hours south to Atlantic City, New Jersey. It wasn't Vegas, but it was closer and had roulette wheels just like they had out in Nevada.

Only, for some reason, the New Jersey roulette wheels didn't spin the same way as the ones out in Vegas.

Instead of winning, Chip kept losing.

In fact, he was down to his last one thousand dollars.

Fortunately, the forty thousand dollars came out of his profits column; it wasn't the bank's money. If he lost a little before this Jersey jaunt was done, the head office wouldn't launch a full-scale embezzlement investigation.

But, losing so much of his own money so rapidly made him feel queasy, like falling down an elevator shaft on a bungee cord. It's why he needed the sick day.

He needed to stay in Atlantic City until he once again had fifty thousand dollars to stow in his desk safe, because Monopoly was no fun if someone came along and took away all your money!

"One hundred on red!" he said, sliding a chip across the felt. If the little silver ball landed in any red-colored number slot, one hundred dollars would turn into two hundred dollars and slowly, but surely, he would begin rebuilding his fortune.

The dealer sent the wheel and ball spinning.

Round and round and round they went.

Until the ball bounced and hopped and skipped and landed in the eleven slot.

"Eleven wins, odd wins, black wins," announced the dealer, raking Chip's chip away.

Chuck Weitzel hated Atlantic City. He hated the whole state of New Jersey. He hated the color red, the number eleven, and the dealer's stupid bow tie because it was red, too!

He was down to his last nine hundred dollars.

He would definitely need a sick day tomorrow.

Because he was feeling ill. Very, *very* ill.

GRANDMA BROWN WAS TUGGING ON the garden hose, pulling it behind her up the muddy path between the dog kennels.

"Quit gawking at me!" she hollered at a trembling beagle puppy with frightened eyes. "Or you don't get any water!"

Riley put down the binoculars, hopped up over the fallen tree, and dashed as quickly and quietly as he could toward the closest dog coops. He flicked on Briana's Flip camera and checked the viewfinder. The digital video recorder was capturing everything: the skeleton-skinny older dogs, the trembling puppies crowded into cramped cages, the extremely unsanitary filth heaped up in the mud below.

Poor Jamal. Unfortunately, he'd have to kneel in the sloppy dog dung to crack open the lock on Noodle's chain. They'd definitely have to make him an official member of the Gnat Pack after heroic service like that.

As planned, Jamal left his hiding place exactly one minute after Riley. He was now creeping stealthily toward his target.

Satisfied that he had all the video he needed to prove that what the Browns were doing was wrong, Riley stuffed the slim video camera into his back pocket and headed for the shed.

Luck was on their side: Chief Brown, intent on winning his Cheese of the Month Club contest, had taken his cell phone for a stroll to some point far, far away.

And Grandma Brown was currently watering the dogs in the far dog hutch, her back turned to the cages where Noodle was chained.

Riley picked up his pace. Trotted toward the shed.

"Oh, you want some of this?" he heard Grandma Brown cackle behind him. "Ha! Here you go! Hehehee!" Riley had to glance over his shoulder to see what the old woman found so funny.

She had her hose nozzle aimed like a pistol at a small French bulldog, its black fur flecked with white. She pulled the trigger and blasted the dog smack on its snout with a gusher that slammed the dog back into the web of chicken wire at the rear of its cage.

The bulldog whimpered. Grandma Brown laughed and laughed, louder and loonier. Then she spit tobacco juice into the crate.

It was time to shut the lights down.

Riley darted behind the post supporting the circuit breaker box. Flipping down his night vision goggles to hide his face, he tried to imitate the high-pitched voice Briana had used when playing Rebecca Drake.

"Hey, lady! Yoo-hoo!"

Startled, Grandma Brown whipped around, her hand still clamped tightly on the nozzle.

"Over here!"

Grandma raised the metal spray gun, aiming to douse Riley like she'd just doused the dog.

Riley leaped sideways, took cover behind the elevated circuit breaker box. Grandma fired a straight stream of water that shot across the kennel yard and hit the bull's-eye: the exposed wiring in the wide-open electrical panel.

Sparks flew. Fireworks erupted. The air smelled like a short-circuiting toaster on top of a pyramid of burning tires.

Then something happened that Riley hadn't planned.

Water being an excellent conductor of electricity, some serious voltage surged upstream to the metal nozzle (metal being another excellent conductor of electricity) and jolted Grandma Brown so hard she zizzed into a seizure—legs thrashing, arms twitching, eyes nearly popping out of her skull—until she finally let go of the hose and toppled, face-first, into the muck.

Oops.

The lights went out.

Somewhere in the distance, Riley heard an explosion and a popping shower of sizzling sparks.

Guess they shorted out the transformer down on the main road, too.

Riley ran over to Grandma Brown to make certain he hadn't accidentally punched out her lights when he knocked out the ones overhead. He raised her wrinkled wrist to feel her pulse. She was unconscious but alive. He tossed her limp arm to the side, where it splatted into a fresh pile of dog poop, courtesy, Riley hoped, of the French bulldog she had just sprayed in the schnozzle.

"Jamal?" Riley called out in an urgent whisper.

"I got Noodle, man."

Riley whipped to his right. It was pitch dark but, thanks to his dad's night vision goggles, he could see Jamal huddled under the dog coop, hugging the birdcage.

"Let's go!"

"I can't see diddly."

Riley grabbed him by the elbow. "I've got you. Come on."

They started running toward the tree line, Riley guiding Jamal around rocks and brambles and bushes.

Behind him, Riley could hear five dozen yelping dogs, begging him to come back and rescue them, too.

"Don't worry," Riley muttered under his breath. "I won't forget you."

"You better not," said Jamal, who thought Riley was talking to him. "I'm running blind here! Coming in on a wing and a prayer!"

They made it to the dirt road and trotted down to the gate.

Briana was waiting for them at the hole in the fence.

"You got Noodle! Fabtastic!"

"Yeah," said Jamal, cradling the puppy's cage in his arms. "I had Riley run what we call a diversionary tactic. He distracted the old biddy in the combat boots while I did what needed to be done with the locks and chains and various technical issues."

"I heard an explosion," said Briana as Jamal passed her the birdcage so he could slip through the fence.

"They had a small electrical problem," said Riley, climbing through the hole after Jamal.

"You got her?" came a happy voice over their earpieces. "You guys rescued Noodle?"

"Yeah, Mongo," said Riley. "Jamal and Briana were awesome!"

"Woo-hoo!" Mongo shouted so loudly into his phone, he nearly pierced everybody's eardrums on the other end.

"We'll swing by your house in fifteen," said Riley.

"I'll meet you guys there!"

"We should take Noodle out of that birdcage, man," said Jamal. "She looks miserable."

"Because she is," cooed Briana, swinging open the tiny door. "Come here, liddle Noodle doodle oodle-baboodle." Baby talk. Another voice Briana had down cold.

Jamal kicked the empty wire birdcage off into the underbrush.

"Jake?" said Riley. "You still on the line?"

"Yeah, Ri?"

"Good work tonight, bro. You were awesome. See you at school tomorrow."

Riley took the Bluetooth device out of his ear and walked up the rutted dirt road with Jamal and Briana, who now had Noodle cuddling in her arms. The happy puppy wouldn't stop slurping its tongue across her face.

"So, what do we tell my mom?" Briana asked between giggles.

"That our friend's lost dog just happened to be

running around in the exact same field we picked for stargazing," said Riley.

"Cool. She'll call it kismet. You know what that word means, Jamal? *Kismet?*"

"No. But I tell you what, Briana Bloomfield: I know how to look it up! It starts with a *K*, am I right?"

When they all laughed, Noodle barked.

It was the first *happy* bark any of them had heard all night.

AT EIGHT A.M. ON MONDAY morning, Otto and Fred, the suburban bank robbers, were sitting behind the tinted windows of their dark-blue van, eating doughnuts and sipping coffee, which was especially difficult for Fred because he had a pair of binoculars glued to his eyes. He kept dribbling mocha-colored drool down the front of his black poplin jacket.

"Not for nothing," said Otto, "but I'm wondering if maybe you should wait on breakfast until after we complete our morning surveillance?"

"Shhh! Here comes somebody."

"The bank manager?"

"No. It's a woman. If memory serves, she's one of

the tellers. The redhead."

"Ah, yes," said Otto. "Window three, I believe."

"You ready for the magic numbers?"

Otto flipped open a tiny spiral notebook. Licked the lead in his stubby pencil. "Fire when ready."

"Two-two-two," said Fred. "Three-three-three. Four-four-four. She's pushing open the rear door."

"That's it? Two-two-two, three-three-three, four-four-four? You're sure?"

"Positive." Fred lowered the binoculars. "And, since I didn't see her insert no key into no keyhole, we can assume the code not only disarms the burglar alarm, it also unlocks the back door."

"Fred?"

"Yes, Otto?"

"This is the lamest security code I have ever seen. It's like Mr. Weitzel, the bank manager, isn't even trying!"

"I concur. Also, the fact that the same code, lame as it is, unlocks the back door seems to indicate Mr. Weitzel takes a very lax attitude toward all security measures."

"Which should make our job on Thursday night even easier."

"Just so long as there ain't no guard dogs," said Fred with a quivering shiver.

"Relax, Fred. Somebody so lazy they make two-

two-two, three-three-three, four-four-four their entry code is gonna be too lazy to even think about hiring guard dogs!"

That same Monday morning at Fairview High School, Gavin Brown was wandering the hallways, searching for the girl of his dreams.

Rebecca Drake!

The perky blond cheerleader. The girl who said she loved Gavin's ripped-sleeve look, which was why he had worn another sleeveless shirt to school. Sure, it made things a little chilly around the armpit hairs and gave everybody a good whiff of his BO, but Gavin didn't care. He was in love.

He was hugging a three-ring binder he had found (and shoplifted) on Sunday. It had the cutest picture of a goldendoodle puppy on its front cover. The binder was pink and the photo of the dog was like one from a froufrou puppy calendar where the dogs all wear ribbons in their hair and pose next to pansies and picnic baskets. But Gavin wasn't embarrassed to be seen walking the halls of FHS holding it close to his heart, no matter how many upperclassmen sniggered at him or called him a wimp.

If he gave this three-ring binder to Rebecca instead of a real dog, maybe he could still become her new boyfriend.

Gavin froze.

"Stupid, stupid, stupid," he muttered. It's what his father always called him. And, this time, his father was right!

No way was a pink three-ring binder with a photo of a curly-haired dog on the cover going to be enough to win over a way-hot cheerleader like Rebecca Drake. Guys were probably giving her three-ring binders and pet calendars and froufrou junk all the time.

To win her heart, Gavin needed to find a real golden-doodle.

That's when he finally put two and two together and got five because he wasn't very good at math: his grandmother ran a very exclusive, very secluded dog ranch called Pampered Pedigree Pooches. She had all sorts of superexpensive purebred puppies (and their mangier, worn-out moms) penned up in her backyard. She only sold them over the internet to out-of-state yuppie types, but maybe she'd make an exception for family.

Gavin tossed the Hello Doggy binder into a trash barrel.

He would talk to his grandmother.

She'd give him a goldendoodle.

Well, she'd sell it to him or let him work it off by stealing more high-tech gear from fifth graders.

So, right after school, he'd head out to PPP.

One way or another, he would give Rebecca Drake the goldendoodle of her dreams!

That same Monday, Grandma Brown sat in her kitchen steaming, and it wasn't because she'd been electrocuted the night before. She was mad.

"Johnny?" she snapped at her son. "You and your cops have to arrest whoever did this to me!"

The chief was busy shoveling spongy scrambled eggs into his face. He just grunted.

"I think it was a woman," said Grandma. "High-pitched voice. Wore goggles so I couldn't see her face. I want her, Johnny. I want her in your jail by midnight tonight!"

"Going to be hard, Ma," the chief said with a mouthful of mashed mush. "We stole the dog first, remember? I can't arrest somebody for stealing what was already stolen, not with all those Lost Dog posters plastered all over town."

"Fine, Fatso. Then we need to buy us a new goldendoodle!"

"Aw, Ma—can't you go back to just selling regular puppies? Beagles and bulldogs and golden retrievers? You did just fine selling regular breeds."

That's when the newly arrived poodle, sitting majestically in his three-foot-tall crate, disdainfully barked his disagreement. Apricot looked like a French king whose curled wig had been dipped in pure gold.

"Are you nuts, Lard Butt?" said Grandma Brown, who kept a long list of insulting names to call her son so she could keep him in line. "We just shelled out nine thousand dollars on a champion purebred poodle!" She spit some tobacco juice into her almost empty coffee cup. "Here's what we do. We call Apricot's breeders. Tell them we need a full-grown female goldendoodle, too. They ship us one first thing tomorrow. We start cranking out puppies."

"A purebred female goldendoodle will cost fifteen hundred dollars, maybe more!"

"So? Go talk to your banker friend. Shake him down for more cash. Meanwhile, starting tonight, we up the security in the kennel to make sure that thieving woman doesn't come back to snatch Apricot."

"Cripes. Now you want me to hire security guards, too?"

"No, Blubber Belly. We get your boy to do it."

"Gavin?"

"Yep. Tell my grandson to pack his toothbrush. Starting tonight, he's sleeping out back with the dogs!"

ON THEIR WAY TO THE Pizza Palace after school, Riley and his crew, including the newest member, Jamal Wilson (they'd made it official during lunch), dropped by Mr. Guy's Pet Supplies on Main Street.

Riley wanted adult verification that what the Browns were doing at the dog ranch was wrong. His dad was still on that secret mission over in Afghanistan. Riley couldn't go to his mom because, well, he had promised her that he would stay away from Gavin and Chief Brown, and now he was contemplating a heist that dragged in yet another Brown, the tobacco-chewing granny who, of course, was also the chief's mother.

Yeah. It was a big ol' Brown mess.

Riley decided that Jenny Grabowski, animal lover, would have to be the go-to grown-up on this one. She looked like she was twenty-one, so she met the basic minimum requirements of adulthood but was young enough to remember what it was like to be a kid in a jam.

As they walked up Main Street, Riley checked out the Mr. Guy's Pet Supplies truck parked at the curb in front of the store. It was big and boxy, its side panels painted stark white. There was a roll-down door in the rear and what looked like a stowaway ramp just above the bumper.

"Jake?"

"Yeah?"

"What's the cargo capacity on that truck?"

"You mean that sixteen-foot 2001 Isuzu HD box van?"

"Yeah. That one."

"Seventy-five hundred pounds. One thousand twenty-four cubic feet."

"Nice," said Riley, who was already hatching the gang's next caper: Operation Doggy Duty.

He turned to Mongo. "Does your mom still buy one hundred pounds of beef at a time and store it all down in that basement freezer?"

"Yeah," said Mongo. "I eat a lot of beef. Hamburgers, steaks, roasts. Rump roasts, chuck roasts, rib roasts—"

174

"Mongo?" said Briana.

"Yes?"

"Some of us are veggies, okay?"

"Right. Sorry."

"Come on," said Riley. "Inside."

The shop was empty except for Ms. Grabowski, who was stocking shelves with cans of cat food.

"Well, hey! Good to see you guys again," she said when she saw who had come through the front door.

"Good to see you, too, Ms. Grabowski," said Riley. "This is Jake and that's Jamal. They weren't with us when we helped you corral those runaways."

"But, yo—we would've helped, too," said Jamal. "Jake and I are what they call altruistic humanitarians. Do you know what those words mean, Ms. Grabowski?"

"Yes. You two have very big hearts."

"How are Amigo and Pepe?" asked Briana.

"Fine. Still available for adoption. If you'd like to visit . . ."

"Maybe later?" said Riley, arching his eyebrows.

"Definitely," said Briana, "because right now, Ms. G., we need you to look at a video clip and tell us whether, in your professional-pet-care-provider and adult-animal-advocate opinion, what we're looking at is a puppy mill."

"A puppy mill?" Ms. Grabowski said the words like they were toxic on her tongue. "Puppy mills are breeding grounds for misery!"

"Then this is probably a puppy mill," said Riley. "Because, I gotta tell you: the dogs sure looked miserable."

He pushed the play button on the Flip camera. The shaky movie he had made while running alongside the dog coops started rolling. The microphone had picked up the dogs' pitiful whimpers and wails.

Ms. Grabowski looked like she might hurl.

"Where exactly is this place?" she asked.

"About fifteen miles from where we're standing right now," said Riley.

Ms. Grabowski closed her eyes. "Enough. Turn it off."

Riley figured she had just seen the old bulldog in the cage closest to the shed, the one with the terrified eyes and a bad case of the shakes.

She took in a long, deep breath. "What do you kids know about puppy mills?"

"Plenty," said Briana. "They're heinous, which is why a bunch of us got together last year in social studies class and signed a Humane Society pledge promising that we would never, ever buy a pet from a pet store or an internet site or even buy pet supplies from any store that also sells puppies!"

"Good for you," said Ms. Grabowski. "Those cute puppies you see out at the mall? They don't always come from very cute or even clean breeding farms. That's why I always say pet adoption is your best option!"

Mongo grinned. He liked a good rhyme.

"There are laws against puppy mills but they're seldom enforced," said Ms. Grabowski. "Maybe if we circulate a petition and take it to the chief of police, he'll go out there and shut this place down."

Riley raised a finger. "Um, Ms. Grabowski?"

"Yes?"

"Chief Brown? Bad idea. It's his mother's operation."

"And," added Briana, "we think he's a partner in the business."

Ms. Grabowski looked astounded. "The police chief's involved with this? That's horrible!"

"Not to mention detestable," said Jamal. "Horrendous, too."

"Ms. Grabowski," said Riley, "would you, as a responsible adult, agree that it would be justifiable for us to go back to this puppy mill facility, say late Wednesday night, and rescue all those dogs?"

"Definitely. But it could be dangerous. Especially since, as you say, the chief is involved. Doesn't he have a gun?"

"Yes, ma'am. Several."

"Bullets, too," added Mongo.

"He might claim you were stealing his mother's property," said Ms. Grabowski. "You could be charged with a very serious felony. He could shoot you for

177

trespassing on private property."

"True," said Riley. "But right is right, even if everyone is against it; and wrong is wrong, even if everyone is for it."

Ms. Grabowski smiled admiringly. "You're a very interesting young man, Riley Mack."

He shrugged. "What can I say? I've got a soft spot for dogs. So, what if, let's say, somebody went out to this puppy mill situation and accidentally opened all the cages and, coincidentally, all the dogs decided to run away and, by further coincidence, these dogs all just happened to run to the same place because maybe they were hungry and this place had food. Would that be considered stealing?"

Ms. Grabowski gave Riley a quizzical look. "What exactly is it you're asking me, Riley?"

Riley bobbed his head toward the door. "Ms. G.— that cargo truck parked out by the curb. Can you drive that thing?"

CHUCK "CALL ME BROKE" WEITZEL had left Atlantic City around one p.m. on Monday.

They kicked him out of the casino because he didn't have any money left and they didn't like him hanging around the all-you-can-eat buffet, digging for scraps of food in the trash barrels. So, they gave him a free bus ticket home and requested that he never come back to AC again.

He went to the bank as soon as he got off the bus because, frankly, he didn't know what else to do. He wasn't just broke, he was brokenhearted.

Head hanging low, he shuffled into the grand marble lobby, thinking about this embezzlement scheme he had heard about in Utah. A bank manager out there drafted cashier's checks on his branch's account and then drove to another nearby branch of the same bank claiming he needed "cash for the vault."

Of course, the bank manager kept all the money for himself. He did it for twenty years before he was caught. *Yes.* That was the new plan! He needed to write a cashier's check and take it over to the First National Bank branch in Cloverdale. But it was past five. The Cloverdale bank would close soon. He had to hurry. He picked up his pace as he passed the teller cages.

"Mr. Weitzel?"

It was Mrs. Mack, looking concerned.

"Maddie," he said with a quick nod.

"What are you doing here?"

"Feeling better. Came in."

He hurried through the Bank Employees Only door and marched to the counting room, where the binder with the cashier's checks was kept under lock and key in a filing cabinet.

"Mr. Weitzel?"

He whipped around. Now it was Joyce slowing him down. The gal from the customer service desk. "I'm glad you're here!" she said. "The chief of police has been calling all day and . . ."

Chief John Brown strode through the door behind her.

"Thought you were sick," he said with a sinister smile.

"Feeling better. Came in."

"Good for you. Say, I wonder if we might step into your office? I have another business proposition to run by you."

"Well, this really isn't the best time for me. How about we powwow first thing tomorrow? Or Wednesday. Wednesday works."

"How about now?"

The bank manager wondered if Chief Brown had friends in Atlantic City, too.

"Sure," he said. "Now sounds good."

He led the way up the hall to his office.

Chief Brown closed the door. "Let me cut to the chase here, Chuck. You need to loan me another two thousand dollars."

"But . . ."

"Surely you can come up with that kind of money. Unless, of course, you lost it all out there in Vegas?"

"Heh-heh-heh. Good one, John." He swiveled toward his computer and started clacking some keys.

He needed to buy some time to think.

"Let me just check the ol' personal piggy bank," he said, adding another "heh-heh-heh."

If the chief was still harping on Las Vegas, that meant he probably didn't know about the more recent disaster down in Atlantic City. Still, Chuck Weitzel wouldn't have two thousand dollars to lend unless he could race over to Cloverdale before six—yes, their website said they were open till six. It was five fifteen. He needed to hurry.

"Did I mention," said the chief, "that I need the money before six p.m.? Got a supplier standing by, ready to ship."

Okay. Now he needed a miracle.

When he shut down the web browser, his computer screen filled with the grid of security camera feeds.

And Chuck Weitzel found his miracle.

He tapped the function key that made an exterior surveillance camera zoom in.

Yes! It was the old lady. The widow. Rada Rollison.

And she was walking down the sidewalk carrying what looked like a cigar box.

She must've found where her dead husband had stashed the rest of his secret retirement fund!

"Will you excuse me, John?"

"But . . ."

"Just need to run up front. Get you your money."

Weitzel bolted out of the office and dashed to the teller room. He had to beat the widow to window three!

"Maddie?" he said, making it sound like "Baddie" so she'd think his head was all stuffed up again.

"Mr. Weitzel?"

"Could you do me a favor?" He sniffled and coughed and blew his nose.

"You sound terrible."

"Relapse. Would you bind rudding over to the drugstore and getting be sub cold bedicine?"

"Well . . ."

"I'll watch your window while you're gone."

"You really should lie down. I can get Brenda to cover—"

"Doe. I insist."

She grabbed her jacket. "I'll be right back." Mrs. Mack headed for the exit at the rear of the building because that door was closer to Morkal's Drugstore.

Chuck smiled.

Maddie never even saw Rada Rollison tottering across the lobby.

"Good afternoon, Mrs. Rollison," he said, pitching his voice slightly higher.

"Hello, Maddie. Good to see you again."

Yep. Blind as a bat.

"Mmmm-hmmm." He figured he should keep his comments short and sweet, let the old biddy think she was dealing with Mrs. Mack.

She hefted the cigar box up to the counter.

"I'd like to put this in my savings account."

"Okeydokey." He sounded like a soprano in an all-boys choir. He took the cigar box and glanced at the deposit slip.

Four thousand dollars!

He propped open the lid and riffled through the bills. It was all there.

"My late husband hid it in the garage. That man was always hiding money. First I found the two thousand in a coffee can, now this. Tomorrow, my son is coming over to help me check under all the mattresses."

Chuck glanced at his watch. He didn't have all day. He let Mrs. Rollison ramble on as he took a ballpoint pen and dragged it over and over the long leg of the number 4 in 4,000 to turn it into a very wide 1.

"All set," he said, handing her the yellow copy, sliding one thousand dollars and the white copy into Mrs. Mack's cash drawer while smoothly slipping the cigar box down the front of his pants.

"Thank you, Maddie. Good seeing you again."

"Um-hmm. Buh-bye, now."

Mrs. Rollison scuffled across the lobby.

About five minutes later, the real Mrs. Mack came back to window three with a white paper bag.

"Here's your medicine, Mr. Weitzel. I hope it helps."

"I'm sure it will. Thank you."

"Feel better."

Oh, he definitely would! He was back in business!

He'd give two of the three thousand dollars still in the cigar box to the blackmailing chief.

He'd keep one thousand for himself. It was more than enough for him to skip around the Monopoly board one more time!

RILEY, JAKE, MONGO, AND BRIANA hustled up the sidewalk toward the Pizza Palace.

Riley had sent Jamal home to start putting together Operation Loot Sting, a scheme Riley had cooked up so the burglarized fifth graders could retrieve all the loot Gavin and his grandmother had stolen from them.

Yep, they were running two operations at once. It would be a very busy week. So Riley didn't even take time to rearrange the letters on the Pizza Palace's sidewalk reader board, even though "Free Drink With Slice" was almost too easy to pass up—"Filched Wiener Skirt" being the most obvious anagram. There just wasn't time to make it happen.

Before they entered the Pizza Palace, they needed a few details for their final script.

"Jake, what'd you dig up?"

Jake swiped his fingers across his smartphone. "Matching that beagle pup through my dad's facial-identification software, I pegged Grandma Brown's internet portal."

Jake's dad was a bigger technogeek than he was. He worked for the federal government crunching top secret, cutting-edge code that did something to keep America safe. His mom? She was a professor of metamathematics, the study of mathematics itself using mathematical methods. Jake had very smart genes.

"It's a dog ranch called Pampered Pedigree Pooches."

"Good work." Riley turned to Briana. "You got your lines down?"

"Totally. But I'll probably do some improv, make it my own."

"I'm sticking to the script," said Mongo, dabbing at the sweat glistening on his brow. Reciting lines always made him nervous so, whenever possible, they tried to keep his lines simple.

"I see Nick inside," said Riley. "Remember, everything we say can and will go directly back to the Browns."

The four of them entered the Pizza Palace and

ambled up to the counter. They placed their orders and carried their slices back to their usual booth. It wasn't long before busboy Nick was hovering near their table again, taking his sweet time cleaning up the trash in the neighboring booth.

Riley touched the right side of his nose with his right index finger.

Mongo glanced at his palm, where he had written his lines with a marker.

"So, Mongo," Riley started, "your mom got Noodle back?"

"Yes. She paid the reward. One thousand dollars."

"To a bounty hunter named Alligator Hide McBride," said Briana, "who is, like, totally awesome. She roams the country helping people find their lost pets. I think they're going to make a movie about her!"

"And now your mom bought Noodle an electric shock collar?" said Riley.

"Yes," said Mongo, using a napkin to blot more sweat from his brow. "She did."

"I hear electric shock collars are awesome," said Jake. "They don't harm the dog, who wears a grounding wire on her front paw, but if a stranger tries to touch the dog and isn't wearing the properly encoded device on his key chain, he gets jolted with over a jillion gigawatts of milliamperes."

"Yes," said Mongo. He glanced at his palm, where

the ink was smearing with sweat. "It's a very effective detergent."

"You mean deterrent?" said Riley.

"Yes. What Riley said."

Now Nick moseyed over to their booth, his bus tray slung against his hip.

"You done with that?" He pointed to Jake's plate, which still had a full slice of Hawaiian pizza sitting on it.

"Um, no."

Nick nodded. "Say, I couldn't help overhearing your conversation."

Riley let a small smirk glide across his face.

"Did your mom really pay somebody one thousand dollars to get back her puppy?"

Mongo nodded like a bobblehead baseball doll.

"Alligator Hide McBride," added Briana. "She's famous."

"Wow," said Nick. "A thousand bucks. That's whacked."

Riley touched the left side of his nose with his left index finger. Time for act 2. Mongo exhaled a giant sigh of relief; Briana was the star of the next bit.

"You think that's whacked," she said. "I have a super-wealthy cousin from Texas and she's coming to town this Wednesday and she says she's heard about this awesome kennel near here called Pampered Pedigree Pooches where they have the most fabtastic puppies

189

and she is willing to spend *ten* thousand dollars for this one beagle she saw on their website."

"Really?" said Nick, dollar signs flashing in his eyes.

"Yunh-huh. Of course, her father won't let her buy a puppy over the internet."

"Why not?"

"Because, in Texas, they like to 'look a man in the eye' when they buy stuff. So, he'll give her ten thousand dollars but only if she can meet the breeder people at Pampered Pedigree Pooches in person."

Riley could see the wheels in Nick's head spinning.

"Isn't that ka-ray-zee?" Briana rattled on. "Ten thousand dollars for a dog? Of course, her father makes billions pumping oil, so ten thousand dollars is probably what they use for toilet paper every day. Just take a stack of bills to the bathroom. . . ."

"You know," said Nick, "I actually know somebody who knows somebody who works at that dog ranch you're talking about."

"No! Way!" said Briana.

"Yep. I could make a few calls. See if a face-to-face could be arranged."

"Fab-tastic! Okay, it has to be an appointment after dark on Wednesday because Beulah's plane doesn't even land until late."

"Beulah?" said Nick.

"That's my cousin. Oh—and this is important—tell

your friend's friend that Beulah has to meet with them inside some sort of house, not the actual kennel."

Nick's expression brightened. "She doesn't want to see the kennels?"

"No way. She has nyctoagoraphobia. She's afraid of the outdoors at night."

"And you swear her father will pay ten thousand dollars for one puppy?"

"Maybe more. In cash!"

"Hang on. I'll make a couple calls."

Fifteen minutes later, Nick handed Briana a napkin with an address scribbled on it.

"It's all set up. Nine o'clock. Wednesday night."

"Great! Will you be there, Nick?"

"Me? No. I don't work there or anything. I just have this friend who has a friend."

Briana batted her eyes. "Fabtastic!"

Riley and his crew spent the rest of Monday and all day Tuesday putting together the final pieces of the plan.

Riley consulted with Ms. Grabowski about equipment needs and learned that her boyfriend, a crazy animal-rights activist named Andrew—who once chained himself to a supermarket lobster tank, demanding that the seafood department set the crustaceans free, and was already planning a protest of the next

Alvin and the Chipmunks movie because it exploited its young rodent stars—was a limo driver out at the airport.

"He'd really like to help you guys out," she said.

Andrew was in.

So was Dr. Langston at the Humane Society. The vet agreed to treat any "sick strays" Ms. Grabowski just happened to find that week, no questions asked.

Meanwhile, Jake set to work figuring out the volumetrics in the back of the Mr. Guy's truck. Then he helped Ms. Grabowski load and outfit it.

Jamal was busy printing up permission slips and take-home announcements for a bogus fifth grade field trip on Saturday.

And Mongo?

He had about fifty pounds of beef to thaw.

WEDNESDAY NIGHT WAS GAVIN BROWN'S third night of dog duty at his grandmother's kennel.

He would be sleeping in a pup tent set up in the path between dog coops. The first two nights, whenever he rolled over in his sleeping bag, the ground underneath the tent squished. It also smelled like dog poop. By morning, so did Gavin. People at school asked him if he was using a new body wash.

But on Wednesday night, Gavin still hadn't worked up the nerve to ask his grandmother to help him find a goldendoodle for Rebecca Drake.

Rebecca.

It was the memory of Rebecca on the sidelines of

the baseball game that kept Gavin going on these long, poop-stinky nights when the five dozen dogs locked in their cages kept whining and whimpering while he tried to fall asleep.

Like a lovesick puppy, he shrugged his shoulders and sighed.

His grandmother came stomping into the dog yard with a plastic-wrapped package of peanut butter crackers. She was wearing some kind of fancy safari outfit, like she worked at a zoo or something. Gavin figured it was her official dog-selling uniform.

"Here's your dinner," she said, chucking him the bright-orange crackers.

"Thanks, Grandma. Why are you dressed like Dora the Explorer?"

"Because tonight I need to look like I actually enjoy working with animals!" She spit a juicy brown loogie at a pile of dog poop under the beagle hutch. "And tonight you need to be extra vigilant!"

"Okay," he said, even though he had no idea what *vigilant* meant.

"Our queen bee arrived this afternoon." His grandma gestured toward a large crate sitting next to the even larger cage holding Apricot.

"Who's the new dog?" he asked.

"Ginger."

"She's pretty."

"She dang well better be. She cost me fifteen hundred bucks."

"Wow. What kind of dog is she? Another poodle?"

"Nope. She's our new goldendoodle."

Gavin felt his heart leap up into his throat.

A goldendoodle!

He couldn't believe his luck! He had just found Rebecca her dog!

"Don't let anyone touch her, and that includes you."

"Yes, Grandma."

That was the first time Gavin Brown ever lied to his grandmother.

Well, the first time that day.

A few hundred yards away, on the other side of the dark trees ringing the secluded puppy mill, Jenny Grabowski backed the Mr. Guy's Pet Supplies truck up the rutted dirt road to the padlocked gate.

Riley, Jamal, and Mongo hopped out of the cab. Yes, it had been a tight fit on the bench seat.

The three guys ran around to the rear of the truck to slide out the loading ramp.

"When I give you the signal, roll up the cargo door," Riley said to Mongo.

"Okay. Can I wear the mask?"

"What mask?"

With a great deal of squeakage, Mongo pulled a

rolled-up rubber Frankenstein mask out of his jeans. "I figured I'd be like Nick when he stole Noodle."

"We're not stealing these dogs," said Riley. "We are simply aiding them in their voluntary flight to freedom."

"Oh." There was a moment of silence. "So, can I wear the mask?"

"Sure, Mongo. Enjoy." Riley turned to Jamal. "You ready to pop open a few cages?"

"Definitely. Only no crawling around underneath this time, hear?"

"Not unless we have to."

"By *we* you mean *you*, right? Cause these are new pants, man."

Riley turned back to Mongo.

"When the dogs go in, help them find a berth."

"Got it." Mongo's voice was muffled because he had put on the Frankenstein mask.

"Try to keep things cozy. No crowding."

That's when Riley's earpiece buzzed.

"This is Riley. Talk to me."

"Riley?"

"Oh, hi, Mom."

"Is that how you always answer your cell?"

"Only when I'm totally psyched about a math problem." He gestured for everybody to stay quiet.

Fortunately, the crickets were cooperating.

"That's why I'm calling. You forgot your math book."

Riley thought quickly. "That's okay. Jake's mom has it."

"Dr. Lowenstein has *MathThematics*?"

"Mom—she's a math professor. She has 'em all."

"You're home by eleven, right?"

"Right. Mr. Lowenstein said he'd give me a ride."

"All right. Study hard. I miss you."

"Miss you, too, Mom."

He thumbed off the call and checked his watch. He had an eleven o'clock curfew because it was Wednesday, a school night. That meant the Gnat Pack, aided by two willing adults, had less than two hours to pull off Operation Doggy Duty. Riley realized being a kid made this caper business a whole lot harder than it probably needed to be.

Now Ms. Grabowski strolled around to the rear of the vehicle. She looked troubled.

"Um, Riley?"

"Yes, Ms. Grabowski."

"That five hundred dollars I took out of the cash register . . ."

"Don't worry. Briana will bring it back."

"Good. Because while Andrew and I are totally happy to help you guys because we both believe in animal rescue—even slightly illegal animal rescue—my boss has no idea we're using his truck or his money or the fact that we're, basically, stealing the police chief's mother's property. . . ."

"I told you: we'll only take the dogs who willingly choose to climb into the back of this truck. And the cash is just a prop to help Briana establish her Texas oil tycoon cred. We won't lose a single bill."

"Right, right. But when can Mr. Guy have his truck back for deliveries?"

"You told him about the gas and brake pedal problems? The recall alert?"

"Yes. I read the whole script you and Briana wrote. He knows we have to keep the truck off the road until the safety inspector comes by to check it out next week."

"Then we're all good," Riley said with great confidence, even though his stomach was churning. This was his biggest operation ever. He had never had this many plates up in the air, spinning on poles, before. He just hoped he wouldn't be spending the rest of his life sweeping up broken dishes if everything came crashing down around him.

"We're good for a week, Riley," said Ms. Grabowski, sounding just about as stressed as Riley felt.

But, he couldn't let it show. The guy running a mission never could. His dad had taught him that, too.

"A week should be all we need, Ms. G." Riley grinned, gave her a jaunty two-finger salute, and snapped his night vision goggles down into place. "Now, if you'll excuse us, Jamal and I have to go accidentally pop open a few locks."

"THERE IT IS!" SAID BRIANA from the backseat of the black stretch limousine.

She figured this was how she'd be riding around Hollywood someday soon. Only she wouldn't have the red chaser lights on the floor. They were kind of tacky and made the limo look like a rolling disco. But she'd definitely keep the free soda and snacks in the fridge.

"You guys? That's four sixty-seven Sweetbriar."

The divider window scrolled down.

"We see it," said Jake, who was riding up front with Andrew, the driver. Jake had a huge battery-powered boom box sitting on his lap.

As they pulled into the gravel driveway, Andrew, a college guy with beatnik facial hair, gave Briana a righteous power-to-the-people fist pump. "Save the puppies, sister!"

"Will do, bro," said Briana.

Jake touched his Bluetooth earpiece. "Riley? We are in position. You ready to rock?"

"Ready," Briana heard Riley's voice leaking out of Jake's ear. She wasn't wearing her Bluetooth. Didn't go with the whole Rich Texas Kid costume.

"You ready, Bree?" asked Jake.

She nodded. Fluffed up her teased-out bubble of big hair. "Let's do this thing."

Porch lights flipped on at the house.

Briana waited for the chauffeur to come around and open her door.

"Miss Bloomfield?" croaked the cranky woman waiting on the stoop.

"Yeah, howdy," she said, straightening her rhinestone-studded cowgirl hat and turning to Andrew. "I'm fixin' to head on up to the house," she drawled. "So y'all jest squat on your spurs a spell, hear?"

Andrew clicked his heels and bowed. The guy was good. A natural.

Briana glided up the crackled walkway to where Grandma Brown eagerly awaited. The old woman was decked out in some kind of khaki outfit with lots of pockets and a pith helmet. Maybe she used to work the Jungle Cruise ride at Disney World.

Briana elegantly extended her hand. "I'm Beulah B. Bloomfield. Might I assume that you are the proprietress of Pampered Pedigree Pooches?"

"That's right."

"Charmed, I'm sure."

"Where are your parents?"

"Oh, Daddy is busy drilling for oil. 'Drill, baby, drill,' as they say."

"And your mother?"

"Shopping for furs and diamonds."

"At night?"

"Yes, ma'am. The stores are a heap less crowded after they're closed to the 'general public.'"

"You bring money, girl?"

"I sure 'nuff did. Shall we step inside? As you might have heard, I suffer from a very severe case of nycto-agoraphobia." She dug into her purse and found a fifty-dollar bill to nervously dab at her brow. "And here I am. Outside. At night. Oh, my. I feel about as jumpy as spit on a skillet."

"This way," said Grandma Brown, her surliness softened by Briana's flash of cash.

"Thank you kindly," said Briana as she strode into the house. The instant the door closed behind her, she knew Jake would slip out of the limo with the boom

202

box and head for the shrubs underneath the big bay windows.

"Can we sit over there, y'all?" Briana gestured toward a sofa pressed up against those windows.

"Sure. Take a load off. I printed out the puppy pages from the website. Put 'em in that binder there on the coffee table."

Briana sat on the couch and opened the hastily tossed-together scrapbook. "Oh, my! So many choices! Why, I don't know whether to scratch my watch or wind my butt."

Suddenly, a very dramatic lady started emoting right outside the window. Actually, she was an opera singer doing an aria by Puccini. When she hit a weird note, the windowpanes rattled.

"*O mio babbino caro . . .*"

"What in blazes is that?" said Grandma Brown.

"Oh, that's just my chauffeur," said Briana, practically shouting. "He loves him a good opera."

"*Mi piace, è bello, bello . . .*"

"Could you tell him to turn it down?"

"Yes, ma'am, I could, but he wouldn't do it. He's deaf as a post. I reckon he listened to too much dadgum opera when he was a young 'un." Briana fished a one-hundred-dollar bill out of her purse, rolled it up tight, and proceeded to pick her teeth with it. This second flash of cash helped Grandma Brown ignore the booming opera music right outside her window.

"Now then," said Briana, tapping the first puppy printout, "tell me about this here poochie. I want to know *every* little thing about him."

"Okay. First off, he's a female."

"Well, feed me nails and call me Rusty."

"Huh?"

"Oh, that's just somethin' we say down in Texas. Go on. Tell me more."

It looked like there were at least fifty pages in the dog book. Briana would ask questions about each and every one of them while Jake pumped opera arias out of his boom box.

They'd keep Grandma Brown busy and unable to hear what Riley and Jamal were doing in the backyard—even when all the caged dogs started barking for joy.

Gavin Brown was the only one near the dog coops at that moment and he stood transfixed, listening to the seriously loud yet hauntingly beautiful music booming from the other side of the house.

"Mi struggo e mi tormento!"

The lady was wailing. It had to be opera. Sometimes, on Saturdays, when no one else was home, Gavin would slip in his earbuds and listen to opera on a stolen iPod he had kept for himself.

"Babbo, pietà, pietà!"

Even though he didn't understand a word, Gavin knew the singer was crazy in love. Opera people always were. And after his phone call from Rebecca Drake, Gavin finally understood how love could make you so crazy you'd do wild things like sing when you could just talk!

He trudged determinedly through the mud to the crate caging the newly arrived goldendoodle.

Yes, Gavin had been a bully and a thief most of his young life.

He had stolen for money. He had stolen for fun.

But tonight would be different.

Tonight, he would steal for love!

RILEY TIED THE NYLON FISHING line around the trunk of a tree, securing it about six inches above the ground.

Hunkered down and moving backward, he unspooled the clear string across the width of the bumpy dirt road.

"You always carry fishing line in your backpack?" asked Jamal as Riley looped the nearly invisible string around a second tree.

"Fishing line and duct tape."

Riley snipped the string with the scissors on his Leatherman pocketknife, tied a quick series of knots, and plucked the fishing line like a guitar string. It was so taut, it thrummed.

"What's that for?" asked Jamal.

"Nothing," said Riley. "Unless, of course, we need it."

An opera singer started wailing in the distance.

"Come on. That's our cue." Riley glanced over his shoulder. Mongo, in his Frankenstein mask, was standing on the other side of the gate, holding on to the handles of a portable ice chest, ready to usher dogs up the ramp and into the truck.

Riley gave him a two-finger salute.

Mongo sort of hoisted the ice chest up in reply. Meat juice sloshed out from under the lid and splattered all over his pants and shirt.

They'd deal with the laundry issues later.

Riley and Jamal hiked briskly up the dark road toward the kennels. They could see the hazy glow of the puppy mill's outdoor lights rimming the tips of the trees. Riley figured Grandma Brown must've rewired her electrical box.

Now he heard heavy footfalls. Mud splashing. Branches whipping against fabric.

Riley tapped Jamal on the shoulder. Hand-gestured to the side of the road. Jamal nodded. They both ducked into the underbrush.

Gavin Brown came trundling around a curve. He was cradling a dog that looked like a bigger version of Noodle in his arms.

"I love you, Rebecca!" he shouted as he ran past. "I lo-ooo-ooove you!" Now he was singing along with the opera diva, making up his own aria.

The instant he was gone, Riley activated his Bluetooth device.

"Mongo?"

"Yeah."

"Gavin Brown is running toward your location. He is carrying a dog. A goldendoodle."

"Did they steal Noodle again?"

"No. This one isn't a puppy. But you've got to stop him before he sees the truck. We need to roll out of here without anyone ID'ing our vehicle."

"Right."

"And Mongo?"

"Yeah?"

"Watch out for the trip wire."

"Is that the clothesline thingy you strung between those two trees?"

"Yes."

"Cool. I'll hop over it."

"Works for me."

Mongo set the cooler down on the ground and, moving as stealthily as a 250-pound moose can, wormed his way through the hole in the fence.

The rubber Frankenstein mask was making him sweat something fierce. A salty droplet plunked into his eyeball. He went blind for a second and then remembered he couldn't close his eyes or else he'd trip over Riley's invisible fishing line.

He blinked his eyes to clear them and, seeing just the hint of a glint near the ground, leaped over the booby trap.

He galloped up the muddy road. His shoes started to squish. His pants, too, because he had sloshed some of the sticky beef juice from the cooler onto his clothes when he waved good-bye to Riley. Mongo smelled like a trotting butcher shop.

He rounded a curve and saw a hulking silhouette trotting toward him.

Gavin Brown. With a dog in his arms.

"I looo-ooove Re-beh-eh-ca!"

Gavin was huffing and puffing, fighting for breath. His personal opera had lost most of its gusto.

The dog squirmed in his arms.

"Hang on, Ginger!" he wheezed. "I'm taking you to Rebecca's house!"

The dog started wiggling and jiggling, like it smelled dinner and wanted to go gobble it down.

That's when Frankenstein leaped out of the bushes

and bopped Gavin in the stomach.

"Ooowww!" Gavin sank to his knees. The sucker punch knocked out what little wind he had left.

The dog hit the ground and immediately leaped up into Frankenstein's arms, where it squiggled itself upside down so it could lick the monster's pant legs.

"Rebecca!" Gavin wailed.

Heartbroken, he slumped face-first into the mud, where he was content to weep like the fat lady in the horned helmet who always sings at the end of an opera because she's lost everything she ever loved.

Riley snapped open his fourth combination lock.

It was easy, once you knew how. Jamal was a good coach.

He let the five sickly pups trapped inside the cage paw at the coop's unlocked door until it swung open. They did it, not him. Riley Mack, being a known trouble-maker, was simply out in the woods having fun playing safecracker. The dogs, shuffling and stumbling at first, then hungry for freedom, jumped out of their elevated hutch, hit the ground, and remembered how to wag their tails.

"You've been practicing, huh, Riley Mack?" said Jamal, who was cracking his tenth lock to Riley's fourth. About forty puppies, some fuzzy, some furry, some prancing on their hind legs, others wiggling their butts off, all amazingly happy, had surrounded Jamal. They were yipping and yapping and jumping up and down like kindergarten kids during recess after a cupcake party.

"Hurry," said Riley. "I don't know how much longer the opera music can drown out all this noise."

One of the puppies, a brown-and-white hound with droopy ears, sniffed along the ground in a straight line to where Riley and Jamal had stashed their backpacks. It started pawing at the zippers, trying to burrow its way into the bags.

"There're only a few more locks left on your side," said Jamal, who had already cleared the far row of cages. "And that big poodle crate over there. You go free that fancy-lookin' dude, I'll crack open the rest of these."

"On it," said Riley as he ran over to the poodle. The dog, a full-grown adult in excellent condition, looked very regal and grand, with tight ringlets of fur on its chest and long, feathery ears. There was a small sign hanging off his cage bars: BARON CHADWICK AMADEUS WELLINGTON APRICOT. CHAMPION SIRE.

"Hold on, handsome. Let me help you check out of this fleabag hotel."

Riley cracked the combination and took off the lock.

The big poodle burst triumphantly through the cage door.

It was so happy to be set free, it howled magnificently at the moon.

A very loud, werewolf-sized howl.

35

BRIANA WAS ONLY UP TO page twelve of Grandma Brown's fifty-page dog scrapbook.

"Now you got me smiling like a jackass eating cactus," she said, slapping her knee. "What's this-here one's name?"

"Calico," said Grandma Brown, somewhat wearily.

"Is she a purebred?"

"Yes. Just like the first eleven you asked me about."

"Well, pardon me for being thorough, but Daddy said if I'm gonna spend twelve thousand dollars on a dog—"

"Twelve thousand?" Grandma Brown was licking her chops again. Well, gumming them.

"Why, yes, ma'am. Shoot, Daddy says I can go as high as fifteen thousand because he wants me to have the best little doggy money can buy!"

"Calico is a chinook," said the revitalized dog dealer. "Very athletic, very—"

A tremendous wolf howl pierced through the cascading warbles of the opera singer.

"That's Apricot!" hissed Grandma Brown.

"I thought you said this one's name was Calico?"

"Wait here." The old lady marched to a tall cupboard. "Something's going on out back."

She popped open a cabinet.

Inside, all Briana could see were rifles, including a very shiny double-barreled shotgun, which Grandma Brown yanked out of its rack. She cracked open the barrel from the stock, slid in two plastic-cased shells, spit some tobacco juice on the very stained rug, grabbed a box of ammo, and stomped toward the back door.

"Hang on, Apricot!" she shouted. "Grandma's coming!"

"Someone's coming!" whispered Jamal.

About fifty or sixty dogs were running around the empty coops in crazy circles now, even the sickly ones—all energized by their newfound freedom.

"Grab your meat!" Riley shouted.

Jamal ran to his backpack.

Riley was about to do the same when he saw the weary French bulldog, the one with black fur speckled white. It stood shivering in its cage, too weak to leap to the ground.

The air exploded.

"I got me a shotgun and a whole heap of shells, Miss Alligator Hide McBride!" shouted Grandma. "I'm gonna pepper your behind with lead, you dadgum dog rustler!"

The angry old lady was still maybe a hundred yards away, but Riley could hear the sharp snap and clink of metal as she worked open the chamber to reload.

Riley needed to run but he couldn't abandon the bulldog.

"Come on," he said, "you're riding with me." He grabbed the trembling little dog, stuffed it into his shirt, and buttoned it up snug. With a wiggling pot-belly, Riley ran over to join Jamal.

Another explosion boomed in the sky behind them.

"Dag," said Jamal. "Grandma's not a very happy camper."

"Yeah." Riley dropped to his knees and shooed away the hound still sniffing furiously at the front flap of his backpack. He and Jamal quickly pulled out two plastic bags stuffed with foil-wrapped cube steaks. Riley had hoped all the wrapping would seal in the scent of meat until it was time to vacate the premises. It had worked.

Except for the hound that had the best sniffer in the class.

"Stuff it in your pockets!" said Riley as he slid the raw beef into his jeans. The cube steaks looked like flat hamburgers rimmed with white fat.

The dogs were going crazy now, splitting into two packs, one for Riley, one for Jamal. The big poodle wanted them both.

"This is so gross, man," groaned Jamal, squishing the slimy beef into his back pockets. "I am burning these pants as soon as I get home."

"What goes on back here?" Grandma shouted in the distance. Riley could barely hear her over the chaotic chorus of barking dogs.

"Run!" he said.

And he and Jamal did.

If the dogs chased after them and escaped from the puppy mill? Well, that was their choice.

Briana heard the explosion in the backyard as she ran down the front porch steps.

"Hurry!" cried Jake, who was tossing his boom box into the back of the limousine.

But Briana saw something she just had to capture on video. She stopped and whipped out her Flip camera.

"Briana? Come on!" Now it was Andrew, the driver, begging her to hurry up.

Briana got the shot and dashed to the driveway.

She tumbled into the back of the limo and slammed the door shut just as another shotgun blast boomed from the backyard.

"Let's book!" she shouted.

"Booking," said Andrew as he jammed the transmission up into reverse. The limo screeched out of Grandma Brown's driveway—backward.

MONGO CHUCKED A SNOWBALL MADE out of ground beef up into the back of the truck.

The big goldendoodle that had been carried by Gavin Brown scampered up the ramp and into the cargo hold. Over the past two days, Ms. Grabowski, Jake, and the extremely clever Jamal had outfitted the interior with fifteen fully equipped dog crates along each side wall. The Mr. Guy's Pet Supplies truck had been transformed into a rolling dormitory of triple-decker bunk beds with double-occupancy accommodations for up to sixty dogs.

The goldendoodle, of its own volition, went into the bottom cage all the way up near the front, which, coincidentally, was where Mongo's first meatball had splattered.

For safety reasons only, Ms. Grabowski, who was working the inside of the box van, latched the cage door shut on the goldendoodle. The dog yapped its approval.

"More meat!" shouted Riley, as he and Jamal skirted into the woods, pursued by a pack of sixty hungry dogs with Apricot, the giant poodle king, in the lead.

Mongo reached into the ice chest and started flinging molded meatballs up into the truck.

The dogs, hearing the wet splats and picking up on the beefy scent, streamed past Riley and Jamal, leaped through the hole in the fence, tore up the gangplank, and found their cages for dinner. Ms. Grabowski was toting a smaller cooler over her shoulder and lobbed meat slabs up into the higher cages. She also gave a boost to any dogs that seemed interested in the upper berths, where steak and ribs were waiting in their food bowls, thanks to Mongo's mom and her jam-packed freezer.

Riley and Jamal ran through the brambles to the back of the truck.

"One more passenger," said Riley, handing off the trembling French bulldog to Ms. Grabowski.

Yes, Riley had "stolen" this dog. It had not run up the ramp of its own free will because, basically, it could barely walk. But no way was Riley leaving the worn-out mom behind to die in Grandma Brown's prison camp. He handed it off to Ms. Grabowski.

"Everybody in?"

"Yeah!" said Mongo.

"We are good to go," added Jamal.

Riley hesitated for a second. All of a sudden, it was weirdly quiet. No more barks. No more yips or yaps. Just the slurping sound of fifty-some dogs feasting on their first meaty meal since forever.

Now what? Riley wondered. He had fifty, maybe sixty dogs. They'd need food again tomorrow. And the next day. And the day after that.

Riley Mack needed yet another plan. A new Operation Something-or-Other. He decided he'd worry about tomorrow on tomorrow because he still had tonight to deal with tonight.

"Let's roll it in and roll 'er down," he said as Ms. Grabowski hopped out of the cargo hold. The three guys slid the ramp back into its storage slot above the bumper. Mongo and Riley each pushed a door panel shut. Jamal slapped on the padlock.

"Andrew just called," Ms. Grabowski reported. "He'll take Briana and Jake straight home."

"Cool," said Riley, waiting while Jamal and then Mongo climbed up into the cab and slid across the bench seat. When his two friends were in, Riley hopped up, grabbed hold of the door, and was about to swing into the seat when he saw something in the truck's side mirror.

Grandma and Gavin Brown. Both of them running as fast as they could up the dirt road. Gavin was toting the shotgun, trying to aim it in midtrot.

"Go!" Riley slapped the roof of the truck. "Go!"

The truck lurched forward.

Riley swung sideways and in.

Mongo reached across both Jamal and Riley to grab the door handle and yanked it shut.

As the door closed, Riley heard one last shotgun blast.

He looked in the side mirror.

Both Browns were sprawled out, facedown in the dirt road.

Riley grinned. He figured Gavin must've squeezed the trigger when he and his grandmother tripped on the invisible fishing line Riley had strung across the road.

"So," said Jamal, "that's why you strung that fishing line, huh?"

"Yeah," said Riley. "I guess so."

Chief Brown received the first enraged phone call from his mother at 10:36 p.m.

"They stole 'em all, Johnny!"

"Who did what?"

"The robbers! They stole every single dog, even Apricot and Ginger!"

Apricot and Ginger. Eleven, almost twelve thousand dollars' worth of dog!

"Did you see who did it?" he asked.

"No. Neither did your lazy, no-good son. Where was he when these criminals slipped in?"

"I don't know, Momma."

"I'll tell you where he was: blubbering in the mud. We could've caught those crooks before they got away if he would've stopped bawling his eyes out two minutes sooner."

"Now, Momma . . ."

"And I had me a customer willing to pay fifteen thousand dollars for a single dadgum puppy. But all the commotion scared her off. I don't think she'll be coming back, neither."

"All right, Momma. Did you see anything? Maybe it was that bounty hunter. The one Nick told us about—Alligator Hide McBride. Maybe she came back for more, figured you were easy pickings."

"They had a truck."

"Okay, Momma, that's good. Did you see the license plate?"

"No, I did not see the license plate! Your stupid son tripped me up and knocked me down before we were close enough to see a thing."

"Well, what about the truck? What did it look like?"

There was a long pause. "It was white. A big white truck."

"That's it?"

"It had four tires."

It didn't get much better after that.

RILEY MADE CURFEW.

At 10:55 p.m., dressed in his pajamas, he went into the bathroom to brush his teeth before going to bed. He brought along a phone so he could call Ms. Grabowski. The gush of water in the sink stopped his mom from hearing his side of the conversation.

Ms. Grabowski told Riley that she'd take the twelve sickest dogs to her friend Dr. Langston's veterinary clinic first thing in the morning.

"So what do we do with the other forty-seven dogs?" she asked. "We can't take them all to the animal shelter. It'll raise all sorts of red flags. Especially if Grandma Brown files a formal complaint with her son and he issues some kind of lost dogs bulletin."

"Okay," said Riley, "how about you host a pet-adoption event at your store?"

"What?"

"You park the truck out front. Decorate it up with balloons and bunting."

"Where am I going to find balloons at this hour?"

"I'll send Mongo an email. His dad is a used car dealer. He'll probably let you borrow his big inflatable gorilla, too."

"Okay."

"And Ms. Grabowski?"

"Yes, Riley?"

"Call a pet food company you're tight with. Tell them you want to wrap your whole truck with one of their big vinyl ads. For free. All they have to do is toss in some free samples to send home with each puppy."

"Riley?"

"Yeah?"

"Why do I want to do that?"

"So your truck doesn't look so white tomorrow. My guess, the only thing the old lady saw before she went belly down in the dirt was a white box van. If you wrap it with a colorful ad . . ."

"It won't match her description! Wow, Riley, you're good at this."

"It's like billiards, Ms. Grabowski. You gotta play

all the angles all the time. Meanwhile, tomorrow at school, Briana and I are going to borrow the video-editing suite from FMS-TV."

"Okay. I won't ask why."

"You don't have to. We do a good job, you'll see it for yourself tomorrow night on the six o'clock news."

"What are you guys going to do?"

"Disincentivize the chief. Take him off our trail."

"What?"

"We're gonna make him want to forget he ever heard about the fifty-nine dogs who ran away from his mommy's puppy mill."

On Thursday at noon, Chief Brown's mother was ruining his lunch with her sixth phone call of the day.

"We need more money! Shake down your banker friend. We need twenty, thirty thousand dollars to start over from scratch."

"I'll try, Momma."

"Don't try, Butterball! Do it!"

The chief sighed and let his gaze drift through the diner's window to Mr. Guy's Pet Supplies across the street. A truck, all decorated up with colorful balloons and banners, pulled up in front of the store. It had a huge ad for puppy food plastered on its side.

"Momma, I gotta go."

* * *

226

Jake Lowenstein saw Chief Brown hike up his belt and cross the street in the middle of the block.

Jake had taken the day off from school to earn "community service credits" by helping Ms. Grabowski set up the truck for the animal-adoption day.

"Uh-oh," said Ms. Grabowski when she saw the police chief jaywalking across the street. "What do we do, now? Where's Riley?"

"School," said Jake, trying to sound as calm and cool as Riley always did. Too bad his voice cracked on the *oo* of *school*.

He noted there was a municipal trash can standing at the curb, pretty close to the folding card table Ms. G. had just set up for her adoption papers and pamphlets. Since Riley was busy with Briana editing video, Jake was on his own. It was his turn to hatch a plan. Fortunately, he had studied with the master: Riley Mack!

"Um, Ms. Grabowski," said Jake, "lure Chief Brown over to the table. I have an idea."

While Ms. Grabowski sat down behind the card table, Jake slunk over to the cab of the truck, where he had stowed his backpack filled with electronic gadgets. Riffling through the wires and remotes and black boxes, he found what he was looking for. He popped open its back and slipped in four double-A batteries before pocketing its slim remote in the front pocket of his hoodie.

"What goes on here, ma'am?" he heard Chief Brown say to Ms. Grabowski.

"Haven't you heard?" said Ms. Grabowski. "Today's our first annual doggy-adoption day!"

Jake strolled up behind Chief Brown and dropped the black plastic box into the trash barrel. The remote control had a range of fifty feet but he didn't want to chance it. So, fighting his nerves, he strolled up to the table and stood right next to Chief Brown, who, he figured, wouldn't recognize Jake as one of Riley Mack's "known troublemakers" because Jake usually worked behind the scenes.

"Where'd you get the dogs?" the chief asked Ms. Grabowski.

"They're all rescues."

"Really?" said Brown, eyeballing the side of the truck hard. It was covered with a big, bright ad for something called Barkley's Organic Puppy Chow. "I'm interested in adopting a dog."

"How wonderful," said Ms. Grabowski.

"Me, too," said Jake.

"Wait your turn, kid. I was here first."

"Yes, sir, officer."

"You don't happen to have a big standard poodle?" the chief asked, leaning on the table. "Maybe one that weighs, oh, sixty, seventy pounds?"

Jake pushed the button on his remote.

The fart machine hidden in the trash can did its thing.

Braaap!

"Whoa," said Jake, waving the air in front of his nose. "Eat beans much, officer?"

"That wasn't me, kid."

Jake stuffed his hands back into the front pocket of his hoodie and bopped the button on the remote. The fart machine ripped off another butt buster. The thing had like fifteen different prerecorded versions of flatulence, each one juicier than the last.

"Whoo," said Ms. Grabowski. "Would you like some Beano, officer? Maybe a little Gas-X?"

"I told you—that wasn't me!"

Jake tapped the hidden button again. The sound effects box sent up a very long-winded trombone solo.

Ms. Grabowski giggled. Chief Brown's face went red.

Another tap, and out came a wet and sloppy rumbler.

"Who's doing that?" the chief demanded.

Jake shrugged—and simultaneously hit the fart button.

This one sounded like it came with a question mark at the end.

"You know, chief," said Ms. Grabowski, using her pet-adoption literature to fan away the imaginary stench, "we don't really open till two, so if you'd like to go find a restroom . . ."

"I don't need a . . ."

Jake saw a slow-moving black sedan pull up in front of the bank. Chief Brown saw it, too.

There was a swirling red light on its dashboard.

Two men in suits and sunglasses climbed out. They adjusted and smoothed their jackets so no one would see what Jake already knew because he watched a lot of movies about spies and secret agents: the two men were carrying sidearms in shoulder holsters.

A third man, also in a suit, but looking more like a shoe salesman than an FBI guy, scampered around the rear of the vehicle to open up a door and help a little old lady climb out of the car.

Chief Brown hiked up his pants again.

"I'll be back later," he said. "Need to see what's going on at the bank."

But first, he turned to Jake and jabbed a pudgy finger at his chest.

"I know what's going on here, kid."

Jake swallowed hard. "You do?"

"Yep. He who smelt it, dealt it!"

ACROSS THE STREET, RILEY'S MOM was finishing up lunch in the break room at the bank.

She'd packed a tuna fish sandwich and an apple. Her friend and coworker Diane was using a napkin to blot grease off the cheese on a slice of pizza she'd picked up at the Pizza Palace. Neither one was interested in the box of doughnuts left over from the morning.

"Oh, Maddie," said Diane, "I meant to ask you: Is Riley going on the field trip this Saturday?"

"I don't think so. What is it?"

Diane found her purse and handed Mrs. Mack a flyer. "It looks pretty interesting. We're supposed to meet all the other kids and parents at the Sherman Green

Flea Market this Saturday at eleven a.m. for a 'History Through Trash and Treasures' lecture at someplace called Grandma's Antiques."

"Oh," said Riley's mom, reading the details at the bottom, "this is for fifth graders. Riley's in seventh."

"Jeff and I are going with Timothy. Sounds like fun."

"Excuse me, ladies." It was Mr. Weitzel, poking his head through the doorway. "Maddie? Do you have a minute?"

"I was just finishing up my lunch."

He beamed his smile. Blinked. "This is important."

"I'll put your sandwich in the fridge for you," said Diane.

"Thanks," said Riley's mom, standing up. "Is everything okay, Chip?"

The smile tightened. "Probably best if you called me Mr. Weitzel today."

"What's wrong?"

He gestured sideways. "Let's talk about this in my office."

"Is Riley okay?"

"Your son? Yes. I mean, as far as I know." He gestured again. "My office?"

"Okay. Sure." She followed him up the hall.

"You have visitors."

"Who?"

"Mrs. Rada Rollison, her son Roger, and two

gentlemen from the Federal Bureau of Investigation's Bank Fraud Division. I didn't catch their names."

He pushed open the door.

Two beefy men in dark-blue suits and sunglasses were standing behind chairs occupied by Mrs. Rollison and a middle-aged man. Mrs. Mack figured the man to be Mrs. Rollison's son. He had her eyes but none of her smile.

One of the suits whipped off his shades.

"Are you Mrs. Madiera Mack?" he asked.

Mrs. Rollison craned her neck like a bird. "Is Maddie here?"

"Yes, Mother."

"Where?"

The son pointed. "Right in front of you."

"Oh. Hello, dearie!"

"Hello, Mrs. Rollison."

"Mrs. Mack?" said the suit.

"Yes?"

"Do you regularly work teller window number three here at the First National Bank of Fairview?"

"Yes."

"Were you working window three on Monday of this week?"

"Yes."

"And is Mrs. Rollison, the elderly woman seated here, a regular customer?"

"I always go to Maddie's window," said Mrs. Rolli-son with grandmotherly pride. "She's the sweetest, the nicest—"

"Ha," grunted her son.

"Sir?" said the second suit. "We talked about this in the car. You need to stay calm."

"Calm? She robbed my mother! If you think I'm going to sit here and say nothing . . ."

Riley's mom was in shock. "I did what?"

The first suit addressed Mrs. Rollison. "Ma'am, did you bring four thousand dollars in cash to this bank on Monday afternoon?"

"Yes. I already told you that. In a cigar box. Remem-ber, Maddie?"

"No."

"Really, dear? You kept the box."

"You also kept three thousand dollars!" added her son.

"What?"

"You're a chintzy, two-bit embezzler is what you are!"

"Mr. Rollison?" Suit two put a hand on the seated man's shoulder. "One more outburst and I *will* be escorting you out of this room."

While Mr. Rollison fumed in his chair, the FBI agent who was apparently in charge showed Riley's mom a plastic evidence bag. Inside the Baggie, she saw a canary-yellow slip of paper.

"This, Mrs. Mack, is the deposit slip for Mrs. Rollison's four thousand dollars. It is dated this past Monday and time-stamped five twenty p.m. Were you working at five twenty on Monday?"

"Bank hours are ten to six Monday through Friday," offered Mr. Weitzel. "Ten to three on Saturdays."

"I was here," said Riley's mom. "But honestly, I don't remember seeing you, Mrs. Rollison. And if you gave me a deposit in a cigar box instead of an envelope, well, I think I'd remember that."

"There, there," said Mrs. Rollison. "Maybe it just slipped your mind, dearie. I know I'm always forgetting things. This morning, I couldn't find my glasses and, wouldn't you know it, I was already wearing them."

"Mom?" sighed her son. "Let the FBI people handle this."

The agent in charge dangled the evidence bag under Mrs. Mack's nose.

"Is that your handwriting?"

"No."

"Did you change Mrs. Rollison's four to a one?"

"Of course not!"

"Well, somebody sure did," huffed the son.

"It wasn't me!"

"Tell it to the judge!"

"Mr. Rollison?" said agent number two. "Let's step outside."

"Let me get the door," said Mr. Weitzel, eager to help.

"Mrs. Mack?" said the agent in charge. "Do you have a lawyer?"

"No, I . . ."

"You should find one. You are under arrest."

"What?"

"You have the right to remain silent."

"I didn't do anything."

"Anything you say can and will be used against you in a court of law."

The room was spinning.

"You have a right to have a lawyer present while you are questioned."

She glanced over to the door. Mr. Weitzel looked so disappointed in her. What about Riley? What would he think?

"I need to call my son. . . ."

"If you cannot afford a lawyer, one will be appointed for you."

"I need to call my son!"

"We'll let you do that from jail," boomed a familiar voice.

There, standing in the corridor outside Mr. Weitzel's office door, was Chief John Brown.

"I figure you boys need to borrow a cell to hold her, am I right?"

"Thank you, chief," said the agent in charge. "Always helpful to have the full cooperation of local law enforcement authorities."

The chief smiled widely. "Happy to help, gentlemen. Happy to help."

OTTO AND FRED, THE SUBURBAN bank robbers, were sitting in a booth near the front windows of the diner on Main Street.

"You see what's going on across the street?" said Fred. "All of a sudden, Thursday is Doggy Adoption Day?"

"You want to go look at the dogs after lunch?" asked Otto.

"Are you kidding?" said Fred. "I hate dogs."

"Yeah. Me, too. That one time I went to prison? German shepherd sent me there. I was working a warehouse job. The security guard was sound asleep, per usual. The guard dog, however, was not. Fritz the fleabag clamps on to my ankle as I'm attempting to boost a giant-screen TV off a storage rack. Dog locks its jaw. Crunches down hard on my fibula like he's munching on a Milk-Bone."

"For me, it was Winky," said Fred.

"Who?"

"Winky. The chow chow that lived next door when I was a kid."

"Chow chow? That the pickled relish?"

"No, it's a Chinese-Mongolian dog breed. Looks like a little puffy lion. Anyways, one summer, I'm maybe five years old. We're in the backyard; my dad's grilling hamburgers. All of a sudden, Winky comes barreling through the bushes, snatches my burger right out of my hand." Fred held up his right hand. "You ever notice my pinkie finger don't have no fingertip? I call it my Winky pinkie."

"Man," said Otto. "I hate dogs."

"Me, too," said Fred.

They were both feeling kind of blue, when they saw an armored car rumble up Main Street, headed for the bank.

"Cheer up," said Otto. "Here comes our money!"

Both men watched the boxy truck pull to a stop in front of the bank.

Two security guards wearing holstered pistols and bulletproof vests came around to the rear of the steel-plated truck, their heads pivoting side to side as they checked the area for any signs of trouble. Satisfied that all was as it should be, the armed goons tapped on the rear door, which quickly swung open. A third goon with a gun hopped out toting several pillow-case-sized sacks of cash.

Otto and Fred were beaming.

It was the weekly shipment of cash in advance of Friday's payday rush at the bank.

And tonight? It would all be theirs!

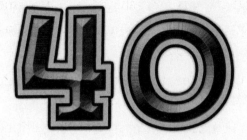

RILEY MARCHED STRAIGHT UP TO Chief Brown's desk.

"Where's my mother?" he asked, very politely, which was remarkable given his current mood.

"Right where the FBI wants her," the chief answered smugly, leaning back in his chair. "In my most secure jail cell."

"Can I see her?"

The chief grinned maliciously. "What's the magic word?"

"Please."

"Please what?"

"Please may I see my mother, Chief Brown?"

"Well, now—at least your bank-robbing momma

taught you a few manners. Or maybe that was your daddy. Where is he anyway? Oh, right. He's way off in Afghanistan, playing soldier with his army buddies. What a shame. Maybe you two should've moved out of town like I suggested."

"Can I please see my mother, Chief Brown?"

"Say 'pretty please' and I'll think about it."

Riley said it. Heck, he'd say anything if it helped get his mother out of this mess. And then? He'd deal with the bullying blowhard police chief. He'd deal with him big-time.

"I didn't do anything, Riley!"

"I know, Mom. But tell me what they *think* you did."

They were sitting side by side on a flimsy cot bolted to a cinderblock wall in a cramped jail cell. The floor was rough gray concrete. A shiny steel sink and toilet were attached to the far wall, only six feet away from the bed. The door was made of solid steel bars. The tiny window, too.

"Did you call the army base?" his mom asked.

"Yeah. They're sending down a lawyer. Guy named Cameron Williams. Dad's friend, General Morgan, says he's the best."

"Good. Thanks."

"Unfortunately, Mr. Williams can't get here till tomorrow morning. He's wrapping up a trial."

"So I have to spend the night in jail?"

"Unless we can come up with fifty thousand dollars in bail money."

"What about you?"

Riley took her hand. "Don't worry about me, Mom. I'll be fine. I can stay over at Mongo's or Jake's."

"Oh, Riley. I wish your dad were here."

"Yeah. Me, too."

His dad's words came ringing back: *"Protect your country, protect your family. . . ."*

Riley's duty was clear: his dad was busy protecting the country. That meant Riley was in charge of protecting his family.

"The more I know," he said, "the more I can do to help."

His mom took a deep breath. "They say I robbed Mrs. Rollison, one of my regular customers. That I took three thousand dollars out of a cigar box and fudged the deposit slip, changed her four thousand into a one thousand."

"She made her deposit in a cigar box?"

"She's a little eccentric. She's also hard of hearing and, I think, legally blind."

"When did you supposedly steal this money?"

"Monday. Five twenty p.m. There was a time stamp on the deposit slip."

"Did they check the security tapes?"

"What?"

"There's a video camera focused on your teller cage to make sure you, or whoever is working window three, isn't taking home any free samples. I saw it the last time I dropped by to bum pizza money."

"Mr. Weitzel didn't mention any security tapes."

"Interesting," said Riley. "Weitzel's the guy with the shiny teeth, right? Always telling people to call him Chip?"

"That's right."

"What's his story?"

His mom shrugged. "I don't know him all that well."

"Good for you," said Riley. "He seems kind of skeevy."

His mom actually smiled. "Skeevy?"

"Simultaneously sketchy and sleazy."

"Then Mr. Weitzel is definitely skeevy."

"Okay," said Riley, "Monday was the day you had to open up the bank in the morning, am I right?"

"That's right. I almost forgot. Mr. Weitzel wasn't feeling well. Said he needed a sick day, even though he did show up for work later that afternoon. Oops."

"What?"

"I forgot to destroy the access code for the back door! I wrote it down on a slip of paper, even though it was ridiculously simple. But I got so busy, I forgot to tear up the code!"

"Where is it?"

"In my purse."

"And where's your purse?"

"They confiscated it out front. Right before Chief Brown took my fingerprints and made me pose for a mug shot."

"Do you remember anything about Monday, late in the afternoon? What were you doing between, let's say, five and closing time?"

"I was working my window and we were busy— we're always busy right after five, people get off work and . . ."

She stopped.

"And what?"

"Mr. Weitzel asked me to run to the drugstore for him!"

A chief's deputy clicked up the corridor.

"Did you do it?"

"Yes!"

The deputy rattled his nightstick against the bars. "Okay, kid. Visiting hours are over."

Riley stood up.

"Don't worry, Mom," he said. "I'll go get you your medicine."

She gave him a very quizzical look, which Riley immediately countered with the slightest head bob toward the guard at the door.

"And then," he said, "we're gonna get you out of

here. I guarantee it!"

"Let's go, kid." The guard held the door open and jerked his head sideways.

"I need to get my mom something out of her purse."

"What? A nail file so she can saw through the bars?"

"No. Her heart medicine. So she doesn't die."

Okay, it was a big fat lie, but it shut the guy up.

And, when they let him rummage through his mom's purse, looking for her heart medicine, Riley was able to palm the access code to the bank's back door.

As for the medicine? That was easy. He sent that deputy back to his mom's cell with a couple white Tic Tacs.

RILEY INFORMED HIS CREW OF his mother's arrest and called an emergency meeting at the Pizza Palace for 4:30 sharp.

First order of business: dealing with Nick the busboy, who was hovering near their booth, again.

"So where'd your cousin go?" he asked Briana.

"Beulah? Oh, she and her daddy packed up their limousine and took their private jet back to Dallas last night."

"They put the limo on a jet?"

"Yes. It's a very big plane. Did I mention how rich they are?"

"Yeah," said Nick, sounding dejected. "But if she still wants a dog . . ."

"She'll totally buy it somewhere else! Did you know that the lady who runs Pampered Pedigree Pooches is a whackadoo? My cousin told me she actually went running into the backyard with a shotgun and started shooting it and stuff!"

"Nick?" shouted Tony, the owner of the Pizza Palace. "Delivery! Now!"

"Well, if she changes her mind . . ."

"Nick?" Tony hollered. "They'd like their pizza while it's hot, huh?"

"Coming," he said, and slumped away from the booth.

"Well done, Briana," said Riley.

"Oh, it'll get better in about ninety minutes," she said.

"You made the drop?"

"Yeah. Dawn Barclay, the investigative reporter at channel twenty-three, and I are tight."

"How come?" Mongo asked innocently. "Does she watch FMS-TV?"

"No, Hubert. That only runs, like, inside the school building?"

"Oh."

"But she visited my language arts class last winter during career day and we totally hit it off. After that, I texted her a few times, gave her a couple makeup tips, helped her de-dorkify her wardrobe, stuff like that.

Anyway, my mom drove me over to the station right after school. I handed Dawn the tape Riley and I edited together, she checked it out and said she wouldn't be surprised if they ran it at six *and* eleven!"

"Excellent." Riley turned to Jamal. "You set for Saturday?"

"Definitely. We are good to go."

"How's Ms. Grabowski doin' with the truck?"

"Six healthy puppies found homes today," reported Jake. "She thinks Saturday will be the busiest day—if we can keep the Browns at bay."

"Oh, we can," said Briana. "Trust me, by this time tomorrow, Chief and Grandma Brown will be pretending they never raised anything on that farm but pumpkins."

"Okay," said Riley. "Now all we have to do is break into the bank."

The Gnat Pack froze.

Jake lowered his hoodie. "I'm sorry, Riley. I don't think we heard you correctly. Did you mention something about breaking into a bank?"

Riley leaned down. His friends leaned in.

"The First National Bank of Fairview," Riley whispered. "Where my mom works. I'm going in there tonight."

"You're a whackadoo, too," Briana whispered back.

"You got delusions of grandeur or something?" added

Jamal. "You know what that means, Riley Mack?"

"Yeah. Means I'm a whackadoo. But don't worry—I know how to disarm the alarm."

"You. Do. Not!" said Briana.

"Yeah. I do. I can waltz in the back door undetected."

Jake raised his hand.

"Yeah?" said Riley.

"Excuse me for asking, but why, exactly, do you want to break into the bank, an act considered illegal in most, if not all, of these United States?"

"I need to locate and copy the security camera recording of teller window three from five twenty p.m. Monday. It'll prove that my mother is innocent!"

And then he gave them all their assignments.

Briana was up first.

She strolled into the bank and found the customer service desk. She hadn't had time to do a complete costume—just some horn-rimmed glasses, her blond wig with a pink bow, and a pink polo sweater tied around her shoulders.

"Excuse me," she said to the slightly distracted woman sitting behind the desk.

"Yes? Can I help you?"

"Golly, I sure hope so," she said, doing her best preppy lockjaw accent. "I'm writing an essay for school on why First National Bank is the best bank in the whole world and I was hoping you could give me a quick tour of your facilities."

"I'm sorry," sighed the woman. "Today isn't a great day for a tour. We've had all sorts of . . . *problems*. Can you come back tomorrow?"

"I could, I suppose, but, gosh, my essay is due tomorrow."

"Well, maybe next time you won't wait until the night before your homework is due to do it!"

Oooh, snap.

"Golly," said Briana. "That's such darn good advice, I must remember to tell Daddy all about you." She opened her notebook and studied the customer service rep's nameplate so she could jot down the name. "Joyce . . . Juzwik. Of course my father, Mr. Franklin Pierce Farnsworth, is the one who suggested I write about his bank instead of the Pizza Palace, which I had originally intended to profile in my report."

"You're Mr. Franklin Farnsworth's daughter?"

"Why, yes," Briana said modestly.

"*The* Mr. Farnsworth? The Chairman and Chief Executive Officer of First National Bancorp?"

Briana waved the fancy title away with a flick of her hand. "I just call him daddykins."

Ms. Juzwik stood up. "Well, Miss Farnsworth, I see no need to disappoint your father. Come on. I'll take you on a tour!"

"Are you certain it isn't an imposition?" said Briana, pulling a digital camera out of her backpack.

"Of course not."

"You're the best, Ms. Juzwik. The absolute best!"

Briana followed the eager young woman around the bank, jotting down notes and snapping pictures of all the stuff Riley said he needed to know and see before he broke in.

CHIEF BROWN AND HIS MOTHER met in the diner at six p.m. for the early bird special.

They took stools at the counter.

"You find my dogs?"

"No, Momma. Been busy."

"Doing what, Lardbreath?"

"Helping the FBI arrest Mrs. Madiera Mack."

The waitress behind the counter turned up the volume on the TV set because the graphic for an upcoming news story had caught her eye: a cute but emaciated dog trapped inside a cage.

"For more on the local puppy mill, we go now to investigative reporter Dawn Barclay. Dawn?"

The screen filled with shaky, handheld images of what looked like a chicken coop filled with barking dogs.

"Hey," said Grandma Brown, "that's my—"

The chief clamped his hand over her mouth to shut her up.

"This nightmarish footage," said the off-camera reporter, "was filmed last night at a local puppy mill called, ironically enough, Pampered Pedigree Pooches."

"How the blazes did the TV people get this footage?" the chief muttered.

"Channel twenty-three received this video from a young investigative reporter who, fearing for her life, has asked to remain anonymous. Our sources inform us that this vile puppy mill operates in the farm country just outside Fairview."

"Eat your dinner, Momma," coached the chief. "Act natural. Stay calm."

"Stay calm? Those are my dadgum dogs!"

"Shhhh!"

"Don't you shush me, Marshmallow Butt!"

The chief stood up from his stool and slapped enough cash on the counter to pay for their meal. "Come on, Momma. We're getting out of here!"

His mother fished her teeth out of the ice water. "Hey," she said, pointing at the TV. "That's my dadgum mailbox!"

The chief glanced up.

There, big as all get-out, was a mailbox with 467 Sweetbriar painted on the side.

The chief dragged his mother toward the door.

"Hurry!"

Maybe it was a good thing all the dogs had been stolen last night. Maybe it was an even better thing that Chief Brown hadn't wasted his day hunting down Alligator Hide McBride or whoever it was that robbed them blind. At least now, when the state's Animal Welfare investigators swarmed the farm, all they'd find would be empty cages.

With empty dog bowls in them.

And petrified dog poop underneath.

"Crap on a cracker! Come on, Mom. We need to go see Old Man Shelby!"

"Why? He's a chicken rancher!"

"Exactly! Maybe he'll sell us some! We need to put something in those cages out back—tonight!"

Meanwhile, Jenny Grabowski was watching the same newscast on a battery-powered TV Jake had set up for her in the back of the pet-supply truck.

She had shut down doggy adoptions for the day and rolled out her sleeping bag in the narrow lane between dog crates. She planned on spending the night with her forty-one remaining rescues, just to make certain they were all watered, fed, and walked.

So, to pass the time, she unfolded a patio chair and watched Briana's big story break on the local news. After the world saw it, no way were Chief or Grandma Brown going to try to take back the dogs they'd been abusing.

"State authorities have assured channel twenty-three that they will soon shut this puppy mill down," said the TV.

"Yes!" Jenny shouted, pumping her fist in the air and howling out a few "Woo-hoos" for good measure.

The dogs agreed.

They howled with her!

RILEY'S CREW RECONVENED AT 6:30 p.m. at Jake's house.

Riley would be going into the bank alone; he couldn't ask his friends to share this particular risk. Breaking into a bank, even if you only intended to steal some digits off a hard drive, was a serious offense.

He did, however, ask them all to help him prep. They met down in Jake's basement, where they had told Jake's absentminded-professor parents they needed to dissect a frog and it might take all night.

First up was Briana with photos and notes from her inside surveillance job at the bank.

"Once you come in the back door, you're in this

break room area. Sink. Refrigerator. Coffeemaker."

"Got it," said Jake, who had found a schematic of the First National Bank of Fairview's floor plan on the internet, posted there by the very proud architectural firm that had done the interior renovations five years ago. "The break room is connected to the workroom that leads to the teller windows, right?"

"Yup."

Jake leaned back in his computer chair. "We are in total synchronicity!"

"Excellent," said Riley. "Thanks, you guys."

"You see the ceiling?" said Briana, showing Riley the next picture. "Okay, there's, like, this security camera aimed right at the door. So, when you go in, be sure to smile."

"You're going to need a balaclava, Riley Mack," said Jamal. "You know what a balaclava is?"

"Those flaky Greek pastries?"

"No, man. You're thinkin' baklava. A *balaclava* is a knit cap that covers your whole face. A mask. Like the wrestlers always wear. Here." He tossed a black woolen cap with four holes in it—eyes, nose, and mouth—to Riley. "I found it in my dad's closet."

"Is your father a professional wrestler?" asked Mongo.

"No, dude. He just wears this when he goes skiing."

"Oh."

"Thanks," said Riley. "Briana?"

"Yeah?"

"Did the break room have a drop-panel ceiling?"

"Yeah. Like in a dentist's office, you know?"

"Perfect. That security camera being near the back door might actually be our lucky break."

"Uh, no. They'll see you, Riley."

"Look," said Riley, "if I'm going to clear my mom, I need to find the security camera footage showing teller window three at five twenty p.m. Monday because I have a sneaking suspicion somebody other than my mother took the cigar box from Mrs. Rollison and monkeyed with her deposit slip. When I find the video recorder, I'll also erase any images it might have captured of me making my entrance."

"The data is most likely on a computer hard drive or a DVR," suggested Jake. "All the closed-circuit camera cables will feed into it."

"Exactly," said Riley. "So, I can climb up on the table in the kitchenette, pop up a ceiling panel, and check out the empty space between the drop ceiling and the real one. That's where they run the air-conditioning ducts, wires, and what I'm looking for: camera cables."

"Cool," said Briana.

"I just follow the cable from that camera, let it lead

me to the mother ship."

"Take your night vision goggles," suggested Briana. "It'll be pitch dark above the ceiling tiles."

"Check!"

"You're going to look like a cyborg in there," joked Jamal. "Ski mask, army-issue goggles . . ."

"And this," said Jake, handing Riley what looked like a jack for a microphone wired to a round gizmo with a tiny antenna. "We should duct-tape it to your goggle harness."

"What is it?" asked Riley.

"World's smallest two-point-four gigahertz micro spy cam. My dad got it for me on my birthday so I could hook it up inside my remote control race car and broadcast a driver's-eye view to the TV. I never got around to wiring it in."

"Why am I wearing a TV camera on my head?" asked Riley.

"So the rest of us can see where you are and what you're doing," answered Briana. "Duh."

"How far does this thing transmit?"

"Not very," said Jake. "We'll hook up the receiver to a TV in the truck."

"What truck?"

"The pet-supplies vehicle."

"With the dogs in the back?"

Jake nodded. "I ran it by Ms. Grabowski. She's spending the night with the dogs and would enjoy the company. I already installed a battery-powered television. We just have to bring our own lawn chairs. Since the truck is parked less than fifty feet from the bank, the signal should come in loud and clear. And, of course, you'll need to wear your Bluetooth earpiece under your balalaika there."

"You mean balaclava," said Jamal. "A balalaika is a Russian guitar."

"You guys?" Riley protested.

"No, he's right," said Briana. "The hat's a balaclava, the guitar's a balalaika."

"No, I mean, I can't drag you into this thing so deep."

"We're fifty feet away," said Jake. "That's not very deep."

"Yeah," said Riley, "in a truck full of stolen dogs."

"*Rescued* dogs," said Jamal. "Come on, man—use your words."

"Riley," said Mongo, placing his beefy hand firmly on his friend's shoulder. "All we are doing is what you would do for any of us."

"But . . ."

"You want me to start squeezing?"

"No."

"All right. Enough said." Mongo released his grip.

"You need me to boost you up to that ceiling?"

"No, thanks. I think I can manage."

"You change your mind, you let me know. I'm not doing anything tonight except watching TV. I hear *The Riley Mack Show* is on."

AT EIGHT P.M., RIGHT ON schedule, Otto and Fred slipped through the back door of the bank.

The code 2-2-2, 3-3-3, 4-4-4 worked like a charm.

Otto tapped Fred on the shoulder and swung his mini flashlight up to the lens of the security camera aimed straight at them as they stepped into what looked like a break room for the bank staff. Otto kept the bright beam of his light glued to the camera lens so all the thing would record was a white-hot circle. Fred hopped up onto the kitchen counter and popped up a ceiling tile.

"Camera cable shoots right."

Otto looked right. "Bathroom."

"Angles ninety degrees."

"Bank manager's office," said Otto.

"Natch," said Fred, gingerly replacing the ceiling tile, hopping down from the countertop—remembering to swipe it clean of any footprints.

The two men had spent several hours over the past week casing the bank. They knew what was on the other side of these walls because they had the layout memorized.

"I'll go erase the hard drive," said Otto.

"You do that," said Fred, flexing his gloved fingers. "I'll go break open the piggy bank."

Fred went right, through the workroom, to the vault. Otto crossed the dark lobby. A little moonlight seeped through the front windows and a couple emergency exit lights cast a faint red glow, but that was it. No one could see the two burglars slinking around in the shadows. Then again, there was nobody to see them because Fairview rolled up its sidewalks early every night. The only vehicle parked on the street was that stupid dog-adoption truck in front of the pet-supplies shop.

Otto made his way to the bank manager's office. He used his picks to pop the dead bolt and a credit card to open the lock in the doorknob. The thing cracked open like the cheap zipper on an even cheaper pair of pants. He stepped in and swung his penlight up the wood-paneled wall to the molding, where he saw a white cable coming down through the ceiling. He traced it all the way to the big man's desk.

Of course, he thought. *The cameras all feed to the boss's personal computer so he can keep an eye on his underlings.*

Otto sat in the comfy leather chair and checked out the glowing monitor sitting to one side of the mahogany desk. The screen was split into a matrix of windows, each one displaying a different camera feed for a few seconds before switching on to a new angle. He could see Fred in the vault room, just past the safe deposit boxes, working on the safe.

Otto pulled out the computer keyboard and started clacking away.

He wasn't in the mood to play nice. So, instead of simply shutting down the cameras and doing an erase going back five minutes to when he and Fred waltzed through the back door, he inserted a software disc that would eliminate all the data files on the bank manager's hard drive. Any pictures of his pets, mother, or girlfriends would be sent to the trash. And not the retrievable trash where the FBI technogeeks could work their data recovery magic and reconstruct them. Nope. Otto was using a souped-up block-erase program to blow the data away.

"Sorry about that, Mr. Weitzel," he mumbled cheerfully. "You ought to be more careful about giving your business card to strangers you meet in a bar."

As he was scrolling through commands, setting up his memory-kill parameters, Otto noticed something peculiar: someone had already erased a chunk of the hard drive's memory. Two hours of video data recorded earlier in the week. Monday. Four p.m. to six p.m. Odd. Very odd.

And they had first exported that two-hour chunk of video to an external drive or removable device.

Even odder.

But not worth worrying about. He and Fred still wanted to be finished in time to catch the local news at eleven. They always did that after a job, usually in a motel at least one hundred miles away from the bank they'd just busted into. They liked knowing whether their handiwork had been discovered.

Otto pressed the final command key and listened to the sweet whir of a hard drive scrubbing itself clean. It took about ten minutes for it to be wiped into oblivion.

He ejected his disc-erasing disc, tucked it into his gym bag, and headed out of the office, shutting the door behind him. The knob locked but he didn't bother jimmying the dead bolt back into place because it was time to help Fred load up the money.

When Otto reached the vault, his partner was still spinning the dial on the safe's combination lock.

"Fred? Is there some problem?"

"Maybe. We got us an Ilco six seventy-three here, Otto."

"So?"

"The Ilco six seventy-three is very testy, very temperamental."

"And?"

"At a recent Safe and Vault Technicians Lock Manipulation Contest in Reno, Nevada—"

"You're making that up."

"Nope. It's a very prestigious event amongst your safe and vault professionals."

"Go on."

"Anyway, the champion—this guy from New Jersey who I met once at my cousin's sister's brother-in-law's—it took him over two hours to crack one of these open. And he was the only guy in the whole competition who could even do it."

"So, what're you telling me here, Fred?"

"One, I can crack this thing. The champ told me a few of his inside moves."

"And two?"

"Nothing," said Fred. "Just that we might not be able to catch the eleven o'clock news tonight."

45

"I'M AT THE BACK DOOR," said Riley.

"We see it," said Jake in his earpiece. "You're coming in five by five."

That meant they were receiving his audio and video signals loud and clear.

"Let's rock and roll," Riley mumbled.

He flipped open the cover on the burglar alarm box and punched in the secret code: 2-2-2, 3-3-3, 4-4-4.

He heard a soft clunk.

"Thanks, Mom," he whispered.

Riley tugged down his ski mask, snapped down the night vision goggles, put his gloved hand on the doorknob, and walked into the bank.

Once inside, he immediately looked up.

There it was, just where Briana said it would be. The security camera.

"Ceiling tile," Jake coached in his ear.

Riley used a chair to climb up on top of the small break room table, careful not to smoosh the half-empty doughnut box still sitting there: he didn't want to leave an imprint of his sneaker on a flattened cruller.

"Going up," he whispered.

He stretched out his arms.

But he couldn't reach the ceiling.

Okay. They hadn't counted on that.

"It seems I'm a few inches too short," he said, refusing to panic.

"I'm coming over there to give you that boost!" he heard Mongo say.

"No!" Riley shot back in a tense whisper. "Give me a minute, here. I'll figure it out."

"Riley?" It was Briana in his ear.

"Yeah?"

"There's a bunch of watercooler bottles over by the sink. They're stacked in plastic crates in the corner on the far side of the counter. If you can put one on top of the table . . ."

"Got it. Thanks."

He stepped off the table to the chair and down to the floor. Thanks to the night vision goggles, Riley could clearly see the tall column of water bottles, each one encased in a hard plastic cube—much better to climb on than the curved sides of a five-gallon jug. This was going to work. Riley went to hoist a bottle off the tower.

It weighed a ton. Fifty, sixty pounds.

No way could he carry it across the room and heave it up on top of the table.

However, he could slide it sideways and watch it drop down to the kitchen counter. He'd climb up and access the ceiling panel from over here.

With a muffled grunt, he shoved the plastic bottle holder sideways and let it fall to the countertop with a heavy, water-sloshing thud.

"What was that?" he heard someone say.

Someone else.

Someone in the bank.

Okay. This was bad.

Riley needed to improvise.

He hopped up onto the counter. Climbed on top of the water bottle and shoved up a ceiling tile.

"How much weight can this ceiling grid hold?" he whispered.

"Not much!" came Jake's reply. "Twenty, thirty pounds."

"Go see what that is," came the voice from the other room.

Riley reset the ceiling tile, jumped down from the

counter, swung open the double cabinet doors under the sink, tossed his backpack into the darkness, then slithered in.

Fortunately, there was nothing stored under the sink except a can of cleanser. He pulled one door shut and, working fast, unzipped his backpack, found his trusty roll of duct tape, peeled off a six-inch piece, doubled it over, and, putting the sticky side to the back of the second cabinet door, pulled it shut.

"What's going on in there, Otto?" he heard the voice call out.

"Nothin'," said a new voice. Gruff. "One of these water jugs here toppled sideways onto the kitchen counter is all."

"You sure it's not a guard dog?"

"Banks do not, typically, employ guard dogs, Fred. They go with retired cops."

"Good," cried the voice in the far-off room. "I freaking hate freaking dogs."

"Me, too. You never know when some German shepherd is gonna want to snack on your shin. For a second, I thought maybe it was the bank manager coming in to watch security camera tapes in his office."

"Why would he wanna do that?"

"'Cause there ain't nothin' else to do in this dumpy little town at night."

"True, true," said his colleague. "Now, can we please

have some quiet? I'm trying to crack open a safe here but I can't hear the tumblers clicking if you keep yakking!"

"All right, already. But hurry up. You're taking forever!"

"I'm hurryin', I'm hurryin'."

Riley heard footsteps walking away. He started breathing again.

"Riley?" Jake in his earpiece. "Where are you? All we see is black."

"I'm underneath the sink," he whispered, quieter than he'd ever whispered before. "We have company."

"Who?"

"Bank robbers."

"What?"

"Stand by. I need to go to Mr. Weitzel's office."

"No, Riley, you need to get out of there. You need to run away."

Believe it or not, when Jake said that, Riley smiled.

"Never run away from danger, my friend. If you do, you only double that danger."

"What?"

"Nothing. Just something my dad says all the time. So, Jake, check your floor plan. Which way to the bank manager's office?"

RILEY WAS CREEPING ALONG QUIETER than a cat hunting a plastic bottle cap.

Jake guided him out of the break room and into what he called the workroom.

"Riley?" It was Briana. "Why don't we call this a dress rehearsal and come back tomorrow night, okay? I think that would be our smartest move, what with the bank robbers and stuff. Okay? Riley? He's not answering me. I hate when boys pretend that they can't hear you. Riley Mack?"

"Easy, Bree," said Jake, keeping his cool. "Let me just keep steering him away from the vault. I assume that's where your bank robbers are currently located?"

"Roger that," Riley whispered.

"Okay. We have a picture again. Try not to talk. Nod for yes. Shake your head for no."

Riley nodded that he understood.

"Okay. That doorway in front of you. Go through it and you're in the lobby. You're wearing sneakers, right?"

Another nod.

"Gumshoe it across the marble at a slight angle to the wall jutting out. Do you see it?"

Riley did.

"The manager's office is on the other side of that small divider."

Riley tiptoed through the lobby. Approached the door.

"That's it. Hurry, Riley."

Riley grabbed the doorknob. It wouldn't turn.

"Is it locked?" asked Jake.

Riley gave him a head bob.

"Okay, Riley Mack." Jamal was taking over back at the truck. "Move closer so I can get a good look at the dead bolt."

Riley moved up to the door.

"We're in luck, man. Looks like somebody forgot to lock it. Crouch down a little lower till you come to where the latch bolt on the doorknob hits the strike plate. There you go. Okay. This is cake, man. You got a credit card?"

Riley shook his head. He was twelve. Banks don't give credit cards to twelve-year-olds.

"What about a knife?"

Yes! He had his trusty little Leatherman with a dozen different blades tucked in his pocket.

"Push a flat blade in there against the angled edge of the latch bolt. Good, good. Jiggle the knife back and forth. You feel the latch? Push it in, man. Push it in!"

Riley did. The door opened.

"I told you it was gonna be cake!"

Riley stepped into Mr. Weitzel's office and silently shut the door behind him. He also quietly cranked the dead bolt back into its locked position.

"I'm in," he whispered, able to speak again since he was behind a closed door. "The security cameras feed to Mr. Weitzel's computer. I heard the robbers talking about it."

"Well, then," said Briana sarcastically, "I'm so glad they got there before you."

"Does his computer have USB ports?" asked Jake.

Riley checked out the sides of the desktop monitor. "Yes. I found two empty slots."

"Excellent. Plug in your memory stick, find what you're looking for, download it, and get the heck out of there!"

"Works for me."

Riley popped his memory stick into a USB connector. He tapped the return button on the keyboard to wake the computer. Nothing happened. He tapped it again.

"Nothing's happening."

"Move your mouse up to the hard disk icon and click it."

Riley did. The hard drive opened into a window.

"It's empty."

"What?"

It hit him. "The robbers. They came in here and erased everything! There are no files left. No security camera footage!"

"Get out, Riley." This time it was Mongo urging him to go. "It's over. You gave it your best shot."

"Mongo's right," said Briana. "Terminate the mission."

"Leave, Riley," pleaded Jake. "Now. Please?"

"It's over, Riley Mack." Even Jamal, the new guy, was chiming in. "Make like a tree and leaf!"

"In a minute," Riley mumbled back.

He sank down into the big leather chair.

He had one last shot to find . . . something. Anything that might help him clear his mother.

He opened the top desk drawer. Nothing but a stapler, paper clips, and several miniature spray bottles of breath freshener. The second drawer was full of fancy-looking stationery and bank forms. That only left the bottom drawer. It was deep. Probably for hanging files.

It didn't matter. Riley needed to check it. If it was nothing but folders stuffed with spreadsheets and memos, then he'd do what everybody was telling him to do: he'd run away and live to scheme another day.

He opened the drawer.

Inside was a hidden, high-tech safe.

"Jamal? You seeing this?"

"Yeah."

"How do I open it?"

"Well, that's what they call a FireKing Executive Safe. See the keypad?"

"Yeah."

"There's only one way to open it: you need to punch in the secret code."

"Okay. How do I figure that out?"

Jamal hesitated. "I don't know."

"Okay."

"I'm sorry, man."

"Get out, Riley," Briana begged. "You'll come up with a new idea tomorrow. You just need to, you know, sleep on it."

"Riley?"

"Yeah, Jamal?"

"Don't mess with that keypad, man. You type the

wrong code three times in a row, the whole thing shuts down, triggers an alarm."

"Which the other gentlemen currently in the bank will undoubtedly hear," added Jake.

"Okay," said Riley, considering all that. "Give me a second."

He had three tries.

What would Mr. Weitzel use as a secret code?

Easy!

The same lame-o code he used for the burglar alarm.

Riley tapped in 2-2-2, 3-3-3, 4-4-4.

Incorrect illuminated on the digital readout.

Okay. One down. Two to go. Riley glanced around the office. Near the edge of the desk, he saw an auto-graphed baseball mounted on a plastic pedestal. Derek Jeter. From the New York Yankees.

Riley tried J-E-T-E-R.

Incorrect.

"Give it up, Riley," urged Jake. "If you get it wrong one more time, alarm bells are going to start ringing."

"Don't worry," said Riley.

"What?"

"I locked the office door."

"Okay, that's enough," said Briana. "Call me a scaredy-cat, call me chicken, call me . . ."

Riley didn't hear what she said after that.

Briana's little rant reminded Riley of what Mr. Chuck

Weitzel told everybody he ever met: "Call me Chip."

Of course.

Riley typed it in.

C-H-I-P.

The lid on the safe popped open.

THE FIRST THING RILEY SAW inside the hardened steel safe was an old cardboard cigar box.

The top was decorated with a painting of six Pilgrim-looking dudes with long, curly locks who looked like maybe they played in a 1980s hair band called The Dutch Masters.

Riley had seen enough cop shows on TV to know how to pry open the lid without smudging any incriminating fingerprints on the box: you use a pencil. He found one in that first desk drawer and eased up the top. Inside was a stack of cash, a slim black book with *Ledger* stamped in gold on its cover, and a USB memory stick with a short note scribbled on its label: "Edit ASAP!!!"

"You guys seeing all this?" he whispered.

"Yeah," said Jake.

"That's the cigar box Mrs. Rollison used for a deposit envelope. There's also some kind of ledger book that maybe records all the money the bank manager skimmed from the till and a memory stick he wants to edit."

"Check it out, Riley!" urged Briana. "Quick!"

"I don't want to touch anything. In case Mr. Weitzel's fingerprints are on the box. Hang on."

Once again, Riley pulled his trusty roll of duct tape out of his backpack. This time, he wrapped a strand around itself at a canted angle, forming a long, thin straw. He bent the tip so there would be a sticky sideways inch at the bottom. Then, working the slender tube of tape down into the open cigar box like a claw game at the video arcade, he snagged the USB flash drive and hoisted it up and out of the desk drawer.

"Got it!"

He didn't care about getting his fingerprints on the device so he picked it up and inserted it into the side of the computer monitor. He moved the mouse and lined up the on-screen arrow with the external drive icon. A quick double click, and the file contents were revealed.

A movie file.

Riley clicked it open.

A grainy black-and-white window opened. It was the raw footage from the security camera aimed at teller window number three. A rolling time display read 4:00 p.m. The motion moved forward herky-jerky style, like the camera was only capturing a frame every ten seconds or so.

"Fast-forward to, like, five twenty!" said Briana. "The bank manager was probably planning on coming in first thing tomorrow, editing out the incriminating scenes, maybe digging up some old footage of the cigar box lady dealing with your mom last week or whatever, cutting it in, faking the time stamp—totally scamming everybody."

Riley nodded. It would take time, but Weitzel could do it.

He kept his mouse on the fast-forward arrows. The video zipped ahead.

"Got it!"

Five twenty p.m.

His mother took a deposit from a male customer in work clothes. He left. Mr. Weitzel joined Riley's mom behind window three. Blew his nose. Pointed to his head. His mom left the teller cage. As soon as she was gone, the bank manager scooted up to the counter— just as a little old lady toddled up to it and handed him a cigar box!

Five twenty-two p.m.

Mr. Weitzel gave the lady a slip of paper. She left. His back to the camera, the bank manager's shoulders shuddered. Having done the front-of-the-pants shoplift move, Riley knew exactly where Weitzel was stowing the cigar box.

Five twenty-nine p.m.

Riley's mom came back carrying a white bag. She handed it to "Chip." He took it and left.

"Bigity-bam!" said Riley. "My mom is totally innocent and this proves it!"

But then a little voice in Riley's head said, *Hang on, pardner.*

He hated when the little voice said that.

You can't just grab the cigar box and go. Even if you show people the security camera movie, they might think your mom and Weitzel were in this thing together, that she had the cigar box at home and told you to go get it.

So what could he do?

Make sure some honest cops find the box and the video clip the same way you found them: in Weitzel's desk!

He needed an exit strategy, a mind-boggling genius scheme that would tie up all the loose ends: the cigar box, the flash drive, the dogs from the puppy mill, everything.

And, of course, he didn't want the bank robbers to

get away or people would think that Riley Mack was the one who had let them in or, worse yet, cracked open the safe in the vault.

Okay. He needed more than a scheme; he needed a grand slam home run.

Think, Riley, think.

"Riley?" said Briana over the earpiece.

"Yeah?"

"Why are you still sitting in the bank manager's office?"

"I need to think."

"About what?" asked Mongo. "You found what you were looking for."

"I know. But the bank robbers complicate things. Just give me another second."

The bank robbers.

They were the biggest variable. Were they armed or unarmed? Did they work at night to avoid confrontation?

All Riley knew about the two men was what he overheard when he was hiding under the sink. They were having trouble cracking open the safe. The guy in the vault sounded extremely grumpy. They knew about the security cameras feeding into the manager's office.

And they hated dogs!

Bigity-bam!

This was going to be, as Jamal called it, cake.

Or, maybe, kibble.

"Guys?" he whispered.

"Yeah?" said Jake.

"I need you to call the number I'm texting you." Riley unclipped his cell phone from his belt, searched the contact list, found his dad's FBI friend. "Contact Larry Chavis. Tell him Colonel Richard Mack's son needs him, that he accidentally got tangled up with some bank robbers."

"I'll do it," said Briana. "I can make it sound real dramatic."

"Wait—Briana?"

"Yeah?"

"When you get off the call with Chavis, contact your news reporter friend. Tell her you've just seen a pack of dogs that look an awful lot like the ones from the puppy mill and they all went running into the bank."

"Oh-kay. But why would I want to tell her a fib like that?"

"It's not going to be a fib for long. Mongo?"

"Yeah?"

"I need you and Jamal to bring as many dogs as you can over to the bank. Use the back door. The access code is two-two-two, three-three-three, four-four-four. Is Ms. Grabowski still there?"

"Yes, Riley?"

"Do you have any treats? We don't have time to send Mongo home for more meat."

"I have a five-gallon tub of Barkley the Baker's bite-size training biscuits."

"Works for me. Jake?"

"Yeah?"

"As soon as the guys send in the dogs, call nine-one-one. If Chief Brown answers, hang up."

"I'll bet he's out at his mother's farm," said Jake. "Helping her cover things up."

"That's what I figure, too. Let's just hope some honest deputies are on duty tonight."

"So," said Mongo, "when do you want us to send in the dogs?"

Suddenly, Riley heard someone outside the door.

"Keep working on it, Fred. I'll check the manager's office. See if he wrote the combination down somewheres."

"Riley?" Jake called through the earpiece.

Riley didn't dare answer. The door rattled in the frame.

"Ah, crap. I thought I left this dead bolt open."

"Riley?" This time it was Mongo in his ear.

He did not answer.

Now Riley heard the click and snick of something thin and sharp working its way into the lock cylinder.

Metal jimmied against metal. The dead bolt started to come alive and slide sideways.

"Riley?" Mongo again. In the background, Riley could hear barking. "When should we bring over the dogs?"

Riley swallowed hard and whispered fast: "Now!"

RILEY FLIPPED UP HIS NIGHT vision goggles, whipped off his ski mask, tugged out his Bluetooth earpiece, wadded everything up—including the micro TV camera—and tossed it all into the wastepaper basket tucked under Mr. Weitzel's desk.

Otto was sliding a credit card down the doorjamb toward the beveled end of the doorknob's latch bolt.

Riley jumped out of the big leather chair, plucked up the USB memory stick with the edge of his shirt, dropped it back into the cigar box, kneed the desk drawer shut, and started pounding his fist on the computer monitor just as the door *oomph*ed open.

"Aw, it's broken!" Riley whined as a man, dressed all in black, stumbled into the office. "Ohmygod! Who are you?"

The man, who had very shiny hair and a dimple in his chin, looked confused. "What? Wait a second. Who are *you*?"

"Charlie Weitzel Junior. This is my father's bank. I think the real question is who the double heck are you? The janitor?"

"Yeah, kid. I'm the freaking janitor."

The guy didn't flash a gun or a lead pipe or any other weapon. Good. That meant he was most likely unarmed.

"What are you doing here so late?"

Riley pointed at the computer. "I came here to play my video game because the bank's fiber optics modem is, like, totally faster than our cable at home, but somebody broke my dad's computer!"

"Your father know you're here, Charlie?"

"Well, duh. How else do you think I got in?"

"He tell you the code for the burglar alarm?"

"Of course he did. He's my dad."

"What is it?"

"Two-two-two, three-three-three, four-four-four."

"Okay. Okay. But, if you're the banker's son, how come there ain't no pictures of you nowheres in this office here?"

"Because I'm too handsome," said Riley without missing a beat.

"What?"

"I'm incredibly good-looking. Whenever other parents see one of my photographs, they realize how plain and ordinary their own children are and that makes them depressed, which means they don't feel much like taking out college loans or mortgages from my dad. My good looks are bad for business."

While the bank robber nodded like he understood the boy's dilemma, Riley checked out the clock nestled in the center of Mr. Weitzel's sterling silver pen set.

Where the heck were Mongo, Jamal, and the dogs?

"So tell me, kid, your father teach you any more secret codes or strings of numbers?"

"Well, let's see. I know his phone number. And the fax number . . ."

"How about the combination to the bank safe? You know that? If you do, I'll know for sure you're the boss's son and then I don't have to call no cops about you breaking in like this."

"I didn't break in and I don't know the combination to the safe."

"This is not what I was hoping to hear, Charlie."

"But," said Riley, "I bet I know where he hides the combination."

"Really?"

"Sure! See, my dad is very forgetful, prone to wool-gathering. Do you know what that word means? *Woolgathering?*"

"He raises sheep as a hobby?"

"No. He's absentminded. Out to lunch." Riley tapped the side of his head. "An airhead, he—"

"I got it, kid, I got it!"

"So, anyway, he hides notes to himself. Always tapes whatever secret stuff he wants to remember to the inside bottom of a cookie jar."

Riley didn't know how much longer he could keep this up.

The robber cocked a thumb over his shoulder. "I saw a cookie jar back there in the kitchenette. Whattaya say you and me go investigate further?"

"Sure!" said Riley, leading the way "I'm starving!"

They marched across the marble lobby and headed into the break room.

"There's the cookie jar, kid."

Riley, standing near the back door, heard the soft thunk of a magnetic lock letting go.

"Dig in!" he said. "The combination will be on the bottom."

The man shoved his hand deep into the jar.

The back door swung open.

Mongo stepped in and side-armed a fistful of dog cookies that went skipping across the floor.

"Fetch!" Riley shouted.

And forty-one frisky dogs, led by seventy-pound Baron von Apricot and his girlfriend, Ginger, came charging into the bank.

"I GOT IT!" SHOUTED FRED from the vault room.

"Dogs!" shouted Otto in the kitchen.

"Dogs?" shouted Fred.

"Dogs!"

Otto dashed across the workroom, just as Jake, Briana, and Jamal came running into the kitchen behind the tail end of the dog pack.

The big poodle in the lead was snarling and snapping at Otto's butt.

"Close the door!" shouted Fred.

"I'm closing it!"

The two bank robbers slammed the door shut.

"Lock it!"

"I'm locking it!"

Riley's crew continued to pelt the vault-room door with dog biscuits. Apparently, they had stuffed their pockets with them. Maybe that was why they took so long.

"You didn't have to bring all the dogs," Riley said to Mongo.

"Yes we did," said Mongo. "Because they all wanted to come."

A mob of barking dogs was clustered outside the vault-room door, gobbling up treats.

"Get these mutts away from us!" shouted one of the bank robbers from behind the door. It was hard for Riley to tell which one it was; his voice was so high and squeaky.

"You okay, Riley Mack?" asked Jamal.

"Yeah. Now." He turned around and saw a dozen or so puppies, bored with barking at the bank robbers, having a field day in the lobby: playing tug with pens chained to writing desks, pulling all the brightly colored forms and slips out of their tidy slots to create an indoor ticker tape parade, peeing on the potted ferns, racing one another around the slick marble floor, jumping on the furniture, chewing on chair legs, sniffing every garbage can they could find.

"Dogs," said Riley. "Nothing but a bunch of trouble-makers. Don't you just love 'em?"

* * *

The local police were the first to arrive on the scene.

The two deputies told Riley that they had been stuck working "the graveyard shift" because "they wouldn't lick Chief Brown's boots."

In other words, they were good guys.

The cops waded through the wagging sea of dogs and persuaded Otto and Fred to surrender after promising to protect them from what the would-be bank robbers called the "mad pack of rabid dogs."

The police puzzled over that description since most of the dogs dancing around in circles or rolling over for tummy rubs seemed to be puppies. But they didn't argue. They stepped into the vault, slapped on the handcuffs, and escorted the two suburban bank bandits through the swarm of dogs.

"Lock us in the back of your car!" begged Fred.

"Hurry!" added Otto, making high choppy steps like he was crossing hot coals. "Don't let Fritz bite my ankle again!"

Fred, the safecracker, had a crazed look in his slightly crossed eyes as he pointed at a fluffy Pomeranian puppy. "It's Winky! It's Winky!"

Chuck "call me Chip" Weitzel, who was notified about the bank robbery as soon as the police received the 911 call, arrived next.

"What the heck happened here?"

"These kids," said the deputy guarding the crime scene while his partner guarded the crooks, "led by young Riley Mack, thwarted a bank robbery. They're heroes. You should give them a reward."

"Is that true?" said Dawn Barclay. The news reporter burst into the bank trailed by her camera crew. Intense spotlight burning bright, they zoomed in on Riley and Briana. "Tell us what happened!"

"Well," said Briana, who loved the limelight, "my friends and I, we were studying when, all of a sudden, we saw this big pack of dogs go running up the street. And we recognized them from your story about the puppy mill!"

"Fascinating," said the reporter, with a wink to let Briana know she wouldn't reveal her as the source for that earlier footage.

"Anyway," said Riley, "we followed the dogs and saw them all come streaming into the back door of the bank because I think some of these dogs are purebred security dog puppies so they instinctively knew something bad was going on in here."

The reporter arched an eyebrow. "Really? The puppies knew the bank was being robbed?"

"Hey, why else would a pack of dogs that just escaped from a puppy mill go running into a bank instead of a steak house?"

"And the back door was propped open," added Jamal, joining Briana and Riley in the bright white circle of light. "Which seemed atypical. Do you know what that word means, Ms. Barclay, *atypical*? Sort of like *asymmetrical*."

While Jamal rattled on, Riley noticed Mr. Weitzel skulking across the lobby toward his office.

"Excuse me," he said. He stepped away from the camera crew and followed "Chip" across the lobby toward his office.

"You can't go in," Mongo said to Weitzel. Riley had stationed his humongous friend in front of the bank manager's door just in case "Chip" got any ideas about making evidence disappear or starting his little editing project early.

"That's my office," said Weitzel.

"Right now," said Riley, "it's a crime scene. See the tape?"

While the cops had been arresting the bank robbers, Riley had strung up all sorts of silver duct tape across Mr. Weitzel's office doorway and written CRIME SCENE DO NOT ENTER on it with a thick-tipped marker.

"A crime scene?" Weitzel scoffed. "Says who?"

"I do," boomed a voice that cut through all the barks and camera crew commotion.

A man wearing a tan trench coat strolled across the lobby, his hands stuffed into the deep pockets. He had a square face and an even squarer haircut.

"And who are you?" asked Weitzel.

"Special Agent Larry Chavis, FBI." He flashed a badge.

Mr. Weitzel flicked on his fake smile and shot out his arm to shake Chavis's hand. "Chuck Weitzel. But you can call me Chip. Pleased to meet you, officer."

Chavis didn't shake Weitzel's hand. He shifted his focus to Riley. "You Colonel Mack's son?"

"Yes, sir."

"How you holding up?"

"Better. Now that you're here."

"Roger that."

"Um, Special Agent?" Now the bank manager sounded all smarmy.

"Sir?"

"Can I bop into my office for a quick little minute? I left some very important paperwork on my desk this afternoon."

"He's lying," said Riley.

"What?" Mr. Weitzel acted offended. "Lying?"

"He wants to go in there and tamper with evidence."

"Special Agent Chavis," said Weitzel, all huffy, "you should know that young Mr. Mack here is a well-known troublemaker around town."

Riley shrugged. "Hey, beats being an embezzler. See, Mr. Chavis, Mr. Weitzel here stole three thousand dollars from one of his depositors, an elderly lady named Mrs. Rollison. Then, he tried to pull a frame job on my mom."

"I did no such thing!"

"Maybe not," said Riley. "I guess the police should search your files, maybe your desk, to see if there is any evidence to support my accusation."

"Good idea," said Chavis. "We'll start with the desk?"

"An excellent choice, sir."

Before Special Agent Chavis could enter the office and find everything Riley knew he would find, Mr. Weitzel lurched toward the door.

Mongo grabbed him by the arm and hoisted him six inches off the ground.

"What's the matter, mister? Can't you read? The duct tape says, 'Do Not Enter!'"

RILEY'S MOM WAS RELEASED FROM her jail cell before eleven p.m.

They needed her bunk for Mr. Weitzel because Otto and Fred were sharing the Fairview Police Department's only other cell.

The chief arrived at headquarters just as Mrs. Mack was being set free. He was covered with chicken feathers. The TV news crews—there were a dozen of them at the police building and outside the bank doing live remotes for their eleven o'clock news broadcasts—all wanted a shot of the chief shaking hands with "the young local heroes."

Forcing a smile, Chief John Brown worked his way

up the line, thanking Briana, Jake, Jamal, and Mongo. When he got to Riley, he leaned in and whispered, through very tight teeth, "This isn't over, Riley Mack."

On Friday, the "Bandit-Busting Bowsers" were all over the news. The *national* news. Briana, who had excellent on-camera skills, did the *Today* show, *Good Morning America*, *Fox & Friends*, *The Early Show*, and about fifteen other interviews by satellite.

The dogs, being doubly famous—first for escaping from a horrid puppy mill and then for courageously confronting the notorious suburban bank robbers— were all adopted by the end of the day. Even the ones recuperating in Dr. Langston's animal hospital would have homes waiting for them as soon as they were treated and released. Briana did a lot of the interviews with her two newly adopted Chihuahuas, Amigo and Pepe, snuggled on her lap.

On Saturday, Riley's mom actually had the day off because starting the following Monday, the people running First National Bank wanted Mrs. Madiera Mack to be the new manager of their Fairview branch. They also wanted to give her a hefty raise and her own office.

Riley and his mom had a big pancake breakfast at the diner to celebrate and decided to go for a stroll.

"We should head over to Sherman Green," suggested Riley. "Check out the antiques."

This surprised his mother. "You like old junk?"

"Depends. I think I'd like it today."

It was a glorious spring day. Flowers were blooming. You didn't even need a jacket. And the sky was the blue people sing about.

"Wow, wonder what's going on over there," said Riley, gesturing toward the crowd gathered outside a triple-tented antiques booth.

"Grandma's Antiques," said his mom, reading the sign. "Oh, a friend of mine at work told me about this. The fifth grade from your school is on a field trip."

"No kidding," said Riley, pretending like he wasn't the one who'd organized the whole fake event. "A field trip?"

"Something to do with studying history through found objects."

"Sounds cool. Let's check it out."

"But you're not a fifth grader."

"True. But I used to be. Come on."

They made their way over to Grandma's Antiques, which was bustling with over a hundred customers. Kids, parents, grandparents.

"Cash only!" snarled Grandma Brown, surly as ever. "You break it, you buy it!"

"Everything's on sale today," added Chief Brown,

302

who, Riley imagined, needed his mom to move a lot of merchandise to make up for all the money they'd lost when Riley's crew, with the able assistance of Ms. Grabowski and her boyfriend, Andrew, shut down their dirty dog business, big-time.

Riley saw Jamal in the tent with his mom and dad.

Jamal raised his eyebrows, waiting for his signal.

Riley touched the right side of his nose with his right index finger.

Jamal smiled. "Yo, Dad—look here. This is my iPod! The one that got stolen at school! Why is Grandma Brown selling my stolen iPod?"

And then the other kids jumped in.

"Look, Mom—it's my Lava Lamp!"

"Hey, she's selling my MP3 recording karaoke player, the one you guys gave me for Chanukah!"

"That's my baseball mitt!"

"My chunky lucky charm bracelet!"

"And this here, dag, it's my other iPod!" shouted Jamal. "Oh, man, this is egregious! Do you know what that word means, Dad? Means this is outrageously bad and unacceptable."

It got better after that.

The parents confronted Grandma Brown, demanding to know why she was selling goods stolen from their children. Several suggested that she needed to be arrested and, since Chief Brown was standing right there, they insisted that he cart his own mother off to jail in handcuffs.

Eager to keep his job and move on before the kids started pointing a finger at his son, Gavin (who was sitting in a corner of the tent with his earbuds stuffed in, singing *"O Sole Mio"*), the chief quickly agreed.

"Mom, you are under arrest."

"What?"

"You have the right to remain silent."

"Take these handcuffs off me, Fatty McFat."

"Okay, that does it. I am sick and tired of you calling me names. I'm locking you up and throwing away the key!"

Riley grinned.

The chief had been so right last night. This thing was definitely not over. In fact, helping Police Chief Brown lose his job was about to move up to the top of the Gnat Pack's To Do list.

Riley and his mom watched the chief cart his snarling mother away.

"So, Riley," his mom asked when they were gone, "how'd you guys really find that security camera footage last night?"

"Sorry, Mom. That information is classified. I'd tell you, but, then, I'd have to shoot you. And, frankly, I love you too much to do that."

His mother laughed and gave Riley a hug.

"I love you, too, you little troublemaker."

That's when her cell phone buzzed.

It was Riley's dad.

He was safe. His whole squad was safe. The secret mission was over and it had been a huge success. Riley's mom and dad chatted for a couple minutes and said a bunch of mushy junk, and then his mom handed the phone to Riley.

"Hey, Dad."

"Riley? How are you?"

"Excellent, Dad. Never better."

"So what'd you do while I was off chasing bad guys?"

"Nothing much," said Riley. "Same old, same old."

"You staying out of trouble?"

"Whenever possible."

And when it wasn't, Riley Mack would do what he did best: he'd protect his family, he'd protect his friends, and he would defend those who could not defend themselves.

And, while he was doing it, he would also do like his dad always said: he would try to enjoy the ride.

THANK YOU . . .

FIRST AND FOREMOST TO MY editors, Laura Arnold and Maria Gomez, as well as editorial director Barbara Lalicki at HarperCollins for assisting me in the development of Riley and his crew.

To Sam and Cameron Morkal-Williams who, years ago, when they were both about Riley's age, first introduced Ms. Lalicki to my writing for younger readers.

To the real Riley Mack for lending me his name. The real Riley, my web maven's son, is a great young guy who has never, ever caused any kind of trouble for anyone anywhere (as far as I know).

To my extremely talented wife, J.J., who has been my first reader/editor on everything I have ever had published. She has an exceptionally keen eye for any boring bits that need to be cut.

To my agent Eric Myers and everybody at the Spieler Agency.

To Riley's art director, Hilary Zarycky, designer Erin Fitzsimmons, and copy editor Kathryn Hinds. Thanks for making young Riley Mack's debut so spectacular.

To the late Donald Westlake and his Dortmunder books for being such an inspiration.

And, most especially, to all of YOU who rescue animals from shelters, take them into your homes, and make them members of your family.